Augustin Daly, Julius Rosen

Needles and Pins

A Comedy of the Present

Augustin Daly, Julius Rosen

Needles and Pins
A Comedy of the Present

ISBN/EAN: 9783743392564

Manufactured in Europe, USA, Canada, Australia, Japa

Cover: Foto ©Andreas Hilbeck / pixelio.de

Manufactured and distributed by brebook publishing software
(www.brebook.com)

Augustin Daly, Julius Rosen

Needles and Pins

NEEDLES AND PINS.

A COMEDY OF THE PRESENT,

IN FOUR ACTS.

(*From the German of Rosen.*)

BY

AUGUSTIN DALY.

AS ACTED AT DALY'S THEATRE FOR THE FIRST TIME,
NOVEMBER 9TH, 1880.

NEW YORK:
PRINTED AS MANUSCRIPT ONLY, FOR THE AUTHOR.
1884.

DRAMATIS PERSONÆ AND ORIGINAL CAST.

MR. NICHOLAS GEAGLE (an elderly party in search of the
   antique and curious in art, comes across a bit of Nature's
   own bric-a-brac, and learns the true reading of an Old
   Nursery Riddle) . . . . Mr. James Lewis
MR. CHRISTOPHER VANDUSEN (a Retired Merchant—
   formerly in "Corks," now in anything but Lavender, who
   cherishes a youthful memory and finds he has been nurs-
   ing a poetic serpent with an unpoetic sting),
                                      Mr. Charles Fisher
KIT VANDUSEN (The dutiful son of the before-mentioned
   Christopher, with his own little secret romance and its
   corresponding consequences) . . . . Mr. John Brand
TOM VERSUS (A spry young Attorney who, not unlike some of
   his elder brethren of the bar, makes a muddle for his soli-
   tary client, while he feathers his own nest) . . Mr. John Drew
SERGEANT MACDONALD, of the 99th Precinct, temporarily
   assigned for duty at the Triton Masquerade . . . Mr. Roberts
JONAH, the superannuated clerk and copyist at Versus' Mr. E. P. Wilks
BLOT, waiter at the Triton Masque . . . . Mr. Beekman
BOX, the porter . . . . Mr. Lawrence

—ALSO—

MRS. VANDUSEN (the home partner of the retired Cork Merchant—full of business in her own sphere—and in fact an
   entire paper of Needles and Pins in her own person),
                                      Miss Fanny Morant
MISS DOSIE HEFFRON (a giddy young thing of —— (date
   missing), who proves to be an unexpected heart breaker
   and an unsuspected syren in unexplored spheres),
                                      Mrs. G. H. Gilbert
SILENA VANDUSEN (her niece, a thorn in her aunt's side,
   though a rosebud in everybody else's sight) . Miss Ada Rehan
MISS MARY FORREST (her first appearance this season. A
   young lady recently come into a fortune; with highly
   romantic ideas as to its disposal) . . . . Miss May Fielding
CAROLINE (a maid servant of the period, and a solemn warning
   to all future Eras) . . . . Miss Maggie Harold
HANNAH, another . . . . Miss Levere

CHARACTERS IN THE MASQUE AND NURSERY COTILLON.

Lahdedah . . . . . Miss Evesson.	Gypsy . . . . . . Miss Shandley.
Captainjenks . . . Miss Kirkland.	The Frog . . . . . Mr. Sterling.
Fanchette . . . . . Miss McNeil.	Januario . . . . . Mr. Bennett.
Gretchen . . . . Miss Donaldson.	Tommydodd . . . . Miss Vinton.
Red Riding Hood . . Miss Flagg.	The Royal Middy . Miss Weaver.
Humpty Dumpty . . . Mr. Wilks.	Aladdin . . . . . Miss Trevalyan.
Robinson Crusoe . . Mr. Lawrence.	Little Bopeep . . . Miss Hinckley.
Champagnecharly . Miss Maxwell.	Mother Goose . . . Miss Brooks.
The Four Dominoes in Black, by	Puss in Boots . . Mr. Macdonough.
Miss Vaughan, Miss Williams,	Bluebeard . . . . . Mr. Hewitt.
Miss Howard, Miss Featherstone.	

Mephistopheles . . . . Mlle. Malvina
        (Under whose directions the dances are given.)

FIRST ACT.

SCENE: The Home of the Vandusens! (By Roberts.)—A suburban house to which the retired Cork-merchant has flown for a Quiet which he does not find. Twenty-five years of the Needles and Pins of Wedlock do not deter two or three more couples from venturing. Three Silenas make their appearance to disturb the calm:—and the fate of the Whisperer is settled.

SECOND ACT.

SCENE: The Law Office of Mr. Tom Versus in this City.—In which the romantic young million-heiress engages her heart, loses her head, and puts her foot in it. The three Silenas turn up in unexpected force to the confusion of several people. A Lesson in Dancing.

THIRD ACT.

SCENE: The Hippodrome Summer Garden decorated for the "Triton" Masquerade. (By Mr. James Roberts.)—Needles and Pins make themselves felt in more bosoms than one: and a Domino Riddle which puzzles the players, places one of them at the mercy of the police. The disastrous results of an exchange of roses and of a sip of spiced Jamaica. One of the Silenas is unmasked and another of them unmasks herself, while the Bric-a-Brac hunter is bereft of his prize. Look up!!

(Incidental to this act will be a duet by Miss Fielding and Mr. Brand and a Chorus and Cotillon of Nursery Rhymes by all the characters.)

FOURTH ACT.

Returns to the Vandusen Mansion and develops sundry headaches and heartaches, after the dissipation and disappointments of the previous evening. A Honeymoon to the Ubjibbelooloo! A new Chinese Puzzle is put together, and the final Silena is quieted at last, while the fable comes to end with a novel rendering of an old Rhyme.

ACT I.

SCENE 1.—*Parlor in pleasant country house near New York. Substantial furniture. Door of entrance* c. *Door* R. *to Mrs. Vandusen's room, and door* L. *to Mr. Vandusen's. Mantel and fire-place* R. 2 E. *Arm-chairs and sofa* L. *Window* L. 2 E. *Small table, with vase, books, etc.*
TIME.—*Winter. Morning.* (*Winter landscape.*) MUSIC.

CAROLINE *enters,* L. C., *with a broom and a bundle of newspapers. Puts newspapers on table.*

Caroline. Lor'! how is it one can be up all night dancing and never feel a bit tired, while a day's work does fatigue one so? What a goloptious time I did have at that ball last night. It was the most genteel ball of the season, it was. I just remember one of 'em: *Him.* "I don't know you to talk to, Miss, but I guess you're Caroline Smith, aren't you?" *Me.* "I guess I am." *Him.* "My sister knew a girl named Caroline. May I dance the next raquette with you?" *Me.* "I guess you may." Oh! it was like a dream. One, two, three and a kick, two and a kick, etc. [*Dances raquette waltz with broom for partner and off* C.]

SILENA VANDUSEN *enters,* L. D., *cautiously.*

Silena. I wonder if my letter's there yet. [*Steals to table and takes a letter from vase.*] Yes, ma didn't discover it. [*Looks at it.*] Its from Gussie at school. She's a happy girl. No mother to find fault and no horrid old aunt to worry. And yet ma don't want me to correspond with her! Because it will make me dissatisfied! So she hunts for letters everywhere. Last night, when I was in bed, she came in to change my pillow, just to see if I had anything hidden under it. What *will* happen when I *do* have a *real* correspondence which she mustn't see. For she thinks I'm nothing but a child, and keeps me four hours a day at the piano, and aunt says I'm a mere chit and ought to wear short skirts. It's just because she's an old maid and wants to keep young herself. Now I know I am *not* a child. I am a young person who ought by rights to dress, go out, shop, make calls and receive attentions. [*About to open letter, goes to* L. *looks off. Conceals it and goes to poke fire,* R.]

MRS. VANDUSEN *enters*, L. D., *in morning costume.   A woman of forty-five, resolute and prompt.*

Mrs. Vandusen.   What are you doing there? [*To Sil.*]
Sil. [*Embarrassed, and rattling the poker between the bars.*]
Fixing the fire, ma.
Mrs. V. Its quite warm enough—look at the thermometer.
Sil. [*Goes to wall,* R. C.]   Why, it's only seventy.
Mrs. V. [*Scrutinizing her.*]   Only seventy!   That's hardly
high enough to account for the color of your face.   Your cheeks
are as red as if you had been found out in something wrong.
Sil. Well, ma, if only a pale face is consistent with a
clear conscience, that accounts for Aunt Dosic powdering so
much.   She'd be turkey-red if she didn't.
Mrs. V. Children shouldn't observe so much, especially
what their elders happen to be doing.   Go and call your father.
[*Crosses to* R.]
Sil. I don't believe pa's up yet.
Mrs. V. I saw him in the garden at the flowers.   Go and
do as I tell you.   [*Haughtily.*]
Sil. [*Affected meekness.*]   Yes, ma, I will go and bring
him to your feet.   [*Exits, laughing,* C. R.]
Mrs. V. That girl is going to give me a great deal or
trouble.   [*Turning.*]   She's growing too fast, and begins to
understand that she's no longer an infant.   [*Goes about, and
looking deliberately at and into everything.*]   If I could only get
my sister off my hands and Kit married to a fortune, I could
devote myself to securing a good *partie* for the child.

SILENA *enters*, C. R., *bringing on* MR. VANDUSEN, *who enters in
morning gown*, C. R., *with watering-pot.   He is a pleasant, easy-
going man of fifty-five.*

Vandusen.   You want me, my dear?
Mrs. V. [R.]   Yes.   Perhaps you are not aware that our
new girl Caroline went to a ball, or a party, or something last
night.
Sil. [*Aside.*]   A ball or a party!   Happy creature!
Van. [C.]   I hope she enjoyed herself.
Mrs. V. No doubt she did, as it was five in the morning
when she came home.
Van.   Then she really must have liked it.
Mrs. V. I gave her permission to stay out till twelve at the
latest.   We must stop this sort of thing at the commencement,
or she'll be spoiled completely.   You will therefore send for her
and give her a good talking to.

Van. Who—I, my dear?

Mrs. V. Yes, you. I don't wish to be always scolding the servants. It gets one the réputation of a fault-finder and termagant, and then one cannot get or keep a decent girl. A few words from a man, on the other hand, will keep the creatures in order without giving the house a bad name.

Van. [*Putting watering-pot off* R. C. *door.*] But, my dear, I don't exactly like to.

Mrs. V. Come! Be a man of inflexible determination for a few minutes. Silena, go and call Caroline. [*Crosses to* C.]

Sil. [*Laughing, and aside, going.*] Papa a person of inflexible determination. I should like to see that. [*Aloud.*] Yes, ma. [*Exits,* C. R.]

Van. I believe it will spoil my whole day.

Mrs. V. [L.] I have laid out my plans, and expect your co-operation. We must live in the country for the sake of economy, and it requires peculiar management to retain good servants.

Van. Well, if you and I are to change places, I think we'd better go back to the city.

Mrs. V. On the means we have?

Van. Oh, business is sure to improve now the election is over.

Mrs. V. At all events we secured a good education for our children.

Van. My dear, you talk as if we were reduced to a final crust.

Mrs. V. It's little better. All my money gone in the fall of coal.

Van. What a pity you didn't put it in ice.

Mrs. V. And now I'm dependent.

Van. On me and Kit. That's only right.

Mrs. V. Hush, here comes the girl. Now be firm. [*Crosses to* R.]

CAROLINE *appears,* C. R. SILENA *follows her and comes down* R.

Caroline. [L. C.] You want me, ma'am?

Mrs. V. Mr. Vandusen has something to say to you.

Car. [*Frightened.*] Mr. Vandusen, ma'am?

Van. [*After sighing deeply, affects a stern air, looks at Caroline, advances a few steps, and slaps the table fiercely.*] Attend to me. [*Folds his arms.*]

Car. [*To Mrs. V.*] Oh, ma'am! what have I done?

Mrs. V. [*Crosses to* C., *and sweetly.*] My child, you had permission to stay out till twelve last night. You exceeded the time by five hours.

Car. It was only three o'clock, ma'am.

Mrs. V. It was five. Was it not, Mr. Vandusen?

Van. [*Thumping table*, R.] Five o'clock!

Mrs. V. [*To Car.*] Mr. Vandusen is dreadfully angry. I have interceded all I can, and if you promise *never* to do it again he will forgive you in the end, I'm sure. [*Going, looks at Van., coughs to brace him up; and exits*, R. *door.*]

Car. Please, sir, it shan't happen again.

Van. Silence! [*Pause.*] Explain yourself! [*She attempts to speak.*] Not a word! [*Looks over his shoulder* R. *to assure himself that Mrs. V. has gone—then pleasantly.*] Did you have a nice time?

Car. Nice time, sir? Oh, at the ball, sir? Oh, it was splendid. I couldn't get away sooner. I was engaged for four quadrilles yet, and three polkas and a schottische—and all with the best dancers, too—and then I thought as you were all in bed, and I wasn't wanted—

Van. [*Reflectively.*] That's a very good point. In fact she was *not* wanted. I don't believe my wife gave that consideration due weight.

Car. Yes, sir!

Van. So you enjoyed yourself, very much?

Car. Oh! very much, sir. They were all young people, sir.

Van. [*Sighs.*] Yes; that is so.

Car. I guess the best way to avoid any trouble in the future, sir, is not to expect me till five o'clock—when I go to a ball.

Van. [*Looks at her.*] Yes, I guess that's the best way. I don't believe my wife thought of that simple solution of the difficulty. You may go, Caroline.

Car. Thank'ee, sir; is that all, sir?

Van. [*Crossing* R., *sits on sofa.*] Yes; I don't think of anything else, at present.

Car. You are very kind, indeed, sir. I'll always come to you instead of to missus, when I want anything. [*Exits*, C. R.]

Van. I don't believe my wife thought of that. [*Turns and sees* SILENA *laughing.*] Oh! you were there.

Silena. [R] Yes, I heard every word. [*Slaps table in imitation.*] Silence! Go on! Not a word! Explain yourself! [*Laughs—advancing.*]

Van. [*Dubiously.*] Was I too rough with her?

Sil. Too rough? I wish mamma had been here; it would have done her good. [*Crosses to* L., *laughing.*]

Van. Well, if she forces me into the housekeeping department, I shall certainly make a mess of it.

Mrs Vandusen *enters* R. *door.*

Mrs. Vandusen. Is she gone? [*To Van.*] The next time you needn't hammer the furniture to pieces. It's no use to overdo a thing. You have probably frightened the girl.

Sil. [*Laughing.*] I'm afraid he has not.

Mrs. V. [*Crosses to* C.] Is that you, my child? I have a word or two to say to you. [VAN. *sits and takes up paper.*]

Sil. [L.] To me, ma? Have I done anything?

Mrs. V. Your aunt has complained of you?

Sil. Aunt Dosie?

Van. [R., *looking up from his paper.*] You are a continual source of irritation to your aunt, my dear, because you are young and she is not.

Mrs. V. She is not too old to have offers, although she has remained single so long.

Sil. I'm sure that's not her fault.

Mrs. V. I see an opportunity now for her to settle—before her chance is altogether gone.

Sil. Pa, how old is aunty?

Van. That is something known only to Heaven and your mother.

Mrs. V. ˙Your aunt, child, is about thirty-five.

Van. [*Reading.*] Reverse the figures.

Mrs. V. [*To Sil.*] Before you came from school, she was the young lady of the family.

Sil. Why didn't you leave me at school?

Mrs. V. Because we could not afford the expense any longer.

Sil. [*Gravely.*] I did not know that. [*To Van.*] What must I do so as not to vex aunty?

Van. [*Reading.*] Grow old and ugly.

Mrs. V. Well, show yourself as little as possible in company till she is married.

Van. [*Same.*] Then good-bye to company forever.

Mrs. V. Keep your very bad jokes for yourself. [*To Sil.*] You ought to keep out of the way of Mr. Geagle, especially. He seems to take a great interest in your aunt. I think she can get him.

Van. What, old Geagle? Ha! ha!

Mrs. V. [*Confidentially to both.*] I have observed him closely. He loves her.

Van. Nonsense. He's merely a bric-a-brac hunter, and runs after anything old and curious.

Mrs. V. For shame, Christopher! [*To Sil.*] Your aunt is a little displeased at his whispering to *you* in corners.

Sil. Yes, but ma, he does so to everybody. Whenever he comes in he sidles up, puts his mouth to your ear, and whispers " Good morning."

Van. The same with me. Took me outside, last Saturday, to remark confidentially that it was going to rain.

Mrs. V. [*To Sil.*] Well, try to keep out of his way until your father has sounded him with respect to his intentions regarding Dosie. [VAN. *jumps up horrified.*]

Sil. Certainly, ma. You may assure Aunt Dosie that I have no designs on Mr. Geagle.

Van. [*Advancing.*] Did I understand you to speak about my sounding Geagle as to his intentions?

Mrs. V. Insinuate to him gently that he's in love.

Van. I suppose he knows his own business best.

Mrs. V. He'll believe whatever you tell him.

Van. My dear, consider. I never did such a thing in my life.

Mrs. V. It's time you learned, then. [VAN. *about to speak.*] Now don't argue the point. I have maturely considered it and it must be done. [*He settles back to his paper.*] Silena, I wish you would call your brother.

Sil. Yes, mamma. [*Going.*] She is full of business this morning. What is Kit to do, I wonder. [*Exits,* C. R.]

Van. [R., *rising and laying aside his paper.*] You must excuse me, this time. Leave me out of the match-making business.

Mrs. V. Now, for Dosie's sake.

Van. Do you want me to make that man wretched for life?

Mrs. V. Dosie hasn't a single bad trait.

Van. With the exception of being a flippant, flirting, finical, foolish woman. If she'd been sober and sensible, she'd have been married long ago.

Mrs. V. Time has softened every fault.

Van. I'll swear it has removed every charm.

Mrs. V. If Mr. Geagle don't see it, there's no harm in encouraging his attentions. He comes up every week, dawdles about her, makes a fool of himself, and her too, and so far it all amounts to nothing. Besides, I must get her out of the way, so I can attend to our own family.

Van. Our own family will get along. Kit has got a capital opening.

Mrs. V. Twelve hundred a year. Just enough to pay for his clothes and cigars. We must find a good match for *him* while he's young and impressionable.

Van. Now, you are not going to shove that poor boy into matrimony by the neck and shoulders.

Mrs. V. I certainly shall not let him miss the chance of a rich wife.

Van. Suppose he won't fall in love with her.

Mrs. V. Nonsense! everybody falls in love with a rich girl.

Van. I differ. All the money in the world will not buy an honest boy's heart.

Mrs. V. Don't talk that way. You are to follow my instructions without question. These are matters peculiarly within the province of a woman.

Van. Exactly, that's why—

Mrs. V. That's why you are to obey implicitly. [*He drops in chair and rubs his head.*] Dosie married, Kit provided for, we shall then be able to settle Silena.

Van. You'll settle them all, I expect.

Mrs. V. Marriage is woman's destiny.

Van. I say, if you get rid of them all, you and I will be left alone. That'll be very lonesome.

Mrs. V. [*Haughtily.*] Thank you for the compliment.

SILENA *enters*, C. R.

Silena. He's coming. [*Comes L.*]

KIT *enters*, C. R., *young man of twenty-three.*

Kit. What is it, mother?

Van. What is it, my son? A mere trifle. Your mother wishes to prepare you for immolation on the altar of mammon or matrimony, which, in this case, is the same thing.

Kit. [R. C.] Matrimony? I?

Mrs. V. [*Severely to Van.*] Mr. Vandusen! [*To Sil.*] Go to your room.

Sil. [*Pettishly.*] What for?

Mrs. V. [*Crosses to her.*] Go this instant. [*Sits down to sew. Sofa L.*]

Sil. [*Going up L.*] But I like to hear secrets. [*Goes up, making a face of discontent, which suddenly clears off. Aside.*] I'll go to papa's room and read my letter. [*Exits gaily, L. D.*]

Kit. [*Sitting on sofa, L.*] Now, mother. Give us a few points about this matrimonial speculation.

Van. [*Seriously.*] Nonsense. It is a mere whim of your mother's.

Mrs. V.   Kit, listen to me attentively.   You have a position with a moderate income.   We sent you to college and to a foreign university at considerable sacrifice.   We have led you to the threshold of fortune.   You must enter by your own exertions.

Kit.   [*Surprised.*]   At considerable sacrifice?   I thought— .

Mrs. V.   Don't interrupt me.

Kit.   I beg pardon.

Mrs. V.   Your father is not in a position to support you and all of us for the balance of his life.

Van.   [*Warmly.*]   My love, I can sustain him until he works into a position of his own.   He is under no necessity of selling himself.

Mrs. V.   Your generosity goes a little too far, my dear. You are beginning to grow old, and yet you have given up many of your accustomed luxuries.   Your club—horses—wines—house in the city—and much more.   I hardly think Kit will consent to further sacrifices of the kind for his sake.

Kit.   [*Rises energetically.*]   Why, mother—father—I'd sooner work at a wheelbarrow—I'd no idea—

Van.   [*Rising, takes Kit's hand.*]   My dear son, this is a little fiction of mamma's.   [*To Mrs. V.*]   You are a very shrewd woman.   You know the boy's weak point—his love for us both—and you would use me as a weight to mould him. [*To Kit.*]   Don't be concerned, my boy.   I gave up luxuries that were really hurtful to a man at my time of life—that's all—

Kit.   [*Takes his hand.*]   Father, the thought of such a possibility would drive me instantly to obey mother in anything she proposes, even if it were repulsive to my sense of honor and independence.

Van.   [*Crosses to Mrs. V.*]   Do you hear what he says? Your plans are repulsive to his sense of honor and independence. For all we know, he may be in love already.   I should be rejoiced to hear that he is.   [*To Kit.*]   Tell me, isn't it so?   You *are* in love.

Kit.   [*Laughing,* R.]   Not exactly.   Although I may say I have been thinking of one young lady a great deal.

Van.   [c.]   Who is she?   What is her name?   Where does she live?   Is she good?   Does she love you in return? But, of course she does.   Well, she must wait for you.   And you will both be unspeakably happy.   [MRS. V. *makes a gesture of despair.*]

Kit.   [R.]   It's impossible for me to answer all the questions. I saw the young lady a year ago, at Silena's school—or rather in that place—at the church.   She played the organ and sang.

We looked at each other—our looks, that is, I can assure you—my looks spoke what I could not utter in words.

Van. She was one of the scholars? [*Rapturously.*] A sweet, innocent school girl?

Kit. [*Hesitating.*] No—o—

Van. Oh, a visitor—a sister of one of the pupils?

Kit. No. I think she was a piano teacher—taken on trial without a salary. [Mrs. V. *makes a gesture of horror.*]

Van. [*Crosses to* R., *less enthusiastic.*] Hem! Hem! Ah! —well, Silena knows her, of course.

Mrs. V. [*Satirically to Van.*] Well, what do you think of it? Does it meet your approval?

Van. [*Crosses to* C., *stoutly.*] I always believe in first love.

Mrs. V. [*Seriously.*] Perhaps you believe a person must necessarily be unhappy who cannot marry his first love. [*With meaning.*] Are you unhappy?

Van. [*Crosses to* R., *uneasy.*] I? What do—why do you ask? What have I to do with it? [*Sitting* R.]

Mrs. V. [*On sofa,* L.] Very well, you can assure Kit confidently that time will heal every wound of that character.

Kit. [*Sitting,* L. C., *next to her.*] Well, mother, have you any particular person in view for me?

Mrs. V. All in good time.

Van. [*Gruffly.*] You had better insert a matrimonial advertisement, or look up a matrimonial bureau—

Mrs. V. [*Dryly.*] I have no doubt it would be an extremely expeditious way of arranging it.

Van. [*To Kit, solemnly.*] Then look out, my son, for the appearance of a marriage broker—a connubial agent—who will introduce you to a customer for one per cent. of the purchase money. There's no telling to what lengths your mother proposes to go.

Mrs. V. [*To Kit.*] It will be time enough for you to know what I propose, when I understand your views of principle in the matter, my son.

Kit. Dispose of me as you please, mother. [*Rises, kisses her forehead.*] My view of principle in the matter is—that I should no longer be a burden here. [*Exits,* C.]

Van. [*Walks up and down in rage.*] A burden! My darling son a burden here! [*To Mrs. V.*] Your cold, calculating, selfish barter and sale of your children is detestable—is wicked—I could—heaven forgive me—I could leave you at this moment and forever.

Mrs. V. [*Lays aside her work.*] I do not doubt it, for you never loved me.

Van. [*Astounded, stops.*] How can you say such a thing!

Mrs. V. Your mother was not very good at keeping a secret. [*Rises.*] She wished me to look upon you as a hero—and so she' told me everything before she died. Everything. [*With meaning.*]

Van. And what was everything?

Mrs. V. That you had been in love with a young girl—a governess—by the name of Silena Summers. You were both young and poor, but full of hope—for you were just attaining a position in life as your son is now, and you were engaged to be married.

Van. [*In low tone.*] Well. [*Sitting near fire*, R.]

Mrs. V. Suddenly your father died, leaving you greatly embarrassed—leaving your mother to your care. You made a proposition to Silena to postpone the wedding, but she insisted on releasing you fully. She said to you, " We dare not wait till your mother's death leaves you free, for as your love for me grew stronger, you might come to look upon that sacred life as a burden. From that hour my love for you would die."

Van. [*Looks up.*] Well, was this girl not worthy any man's affection?

Mrs. V. I have not finished. You parted. After a little while you met me. It was your mother's wish that you should marry me—and you did.

Van. [*Quickly.*] Because I loved you.

Mrs. V. Is it true? Tell me then—why did you call your daughter Silena, if you desired to forget Silena Summers?

Van. [*Rises.*] Have I not been a good husband?

Mrs. V. To be sure you have, and I should have been per-perfectly happy if your mother had only kept her secret to herself.

Van. [*Embarrassed.*] But you don't suppose for a moment that I still think of Sil—of my youthful nonsense?

Mrs. V. Memories are dangerous things. They are the only ones that grow more beautiful with age.

Van. My dear. I have no longer any eye for beauty. The tooth of time—ah! [*Sits at fire.*]

Mrs. V. Gnaws away our defences and lets in the enemy. But don't be uneasy, I'm a practical woman, and know I've no cause for jealousy.

Van. Jealousy at our age!

Mrs. V. Where there is love there is always jealousy. Age has nothing to do with it. *You*, I dare say, are *not* jealous.

Van. Now, my dear, do you want me to make you a declaration of love?

Mrs. V. Not at all. I only wish you to study the happiness of yourself and your children. Do you really believe Kit will be unhappy because he marries a wife of his mother's choice? Didn't you? And are you unhappy?

Van. [*Rising, gallantly.*] Nonsense. Why should I be unhappy? Just the reverse. I am happy. [*Gives her his hand.*]

Mrs. V. Thank you! I was sure you would be sensible. [*Exits,* R. D.]

Van. [*Looks after her.*] She's a good woman. If she didn't have such a genius for managing everybody. [*Thoughtfully.*] So she knew the story of my youth—and never spoke of it till to-day—when I opposed her plans about Kit. But I've done nothing wrong, perhaps. Yet the recollection of Silena was always a pleasant memory. A shrine to which I fled for repose, after a connubial storm. Yes it was right to expose it, to tear away the veil, to shatter the idol, to close the shrine, and I'm glad she did it. But I would like to get in a devil of a rage with somebody. [*Walks up and down; sees Silena off* L.] Silena! What letter is that you are concealing?

Sil. [*Behind scene,* L. D.] What letter, papa?

Van. Come out here.

SILENA *enters,* L., *embarrassed.*

Silena. Here I am, papa.

Van. I saw quite plainly, that you put a letter in your pocket.

Sil. [*Takes out letter.*] I wouldn't have hidden it from you. I was only afraid of mamma. It's only from Gussie Archer at school—and it makes the tears come into my eyes to read it.

Van. Indeed, what does she say?

Sil. Sit down and I'll read it to you. [*Sits at his side, he* C.]

Van. Yes, read it, it will divert my thoughts.

Sil. [*Reads.*] "Dear Silena:—You remember our piano teacher, Miss Forrest, whom everybody liked so much? She has inherited an immense fortune from a very distant relative—half a million they say. She gave a dinner before she left to all the teachers and to six of the biggest girls. It was delicious. She is very romantic and is going to do ever so much good with her money; to help the struggling and to unite those who are victims of disappointed hopes. She spoke particularly of a pair of young lovers she had heard of—a real true story. It seems there was a lovely young girl of eighteen named Silena—just like you—and who taught music. She was beloved by a splendid young fellow named Christopher, just making his way in the world. While they were anticipating with the deepest happiness the day of their marriage, his father died and left him and his mother in the deepest poverty." [*Feeling a tear drop on her hand she looks up and sees him weeping, his head resting on his hand, which is pressed to his eyes; he had listened attentively at first, then becomes deeply moved.*] Papa, what is the matter, are you ill? [*Puts letter on desk behind her.*]

Van. [*Pressing her head to his breast.*] My dear child.

Sil. Shall I call mamma?

Van. [*Holding her to him.*] No! don't call anybody. I am perfectly well. There! it's all right. [*Kisses her, puts her off his knee, rises.*] I'll take a walk in the garden, that will do me good. [*Exits,* C. R., *after kissing her forehead.*]

Sil. [L.] What is the matter with papa? I never saw him that way. I hadn't got to the sentimental part of the story, and yet it was too much for him. [C.]

CAROLINE *enters,* C. L., *with card.*

Caroline. This gentleman wants to see a member of the family, Miss.

Sil. [*Takes cards, reads.*] "Thomas Versus, Attorney and Counsellor-at-Law." Whom does he wish to see?

Car. Guess anybody 'll do, Miss; he said he wasn't particular so long as they was *composentus* and could testify ineligibly.

Sil. [*Puts card and letter on table.*] Ask him in, Caroline.

Car. Yes, Miss. [*Exits,* C.]

Sil. I don't believe papa wants to see anybody and mamma's up stairs. I wonder if he's a country lawyer. [*Looks off* C. *and returns.*] Oh, no; he's city. [*Stage* L.]

TOM VERSUS *enters,* C. L., *hat in hand, is young, lively, well-dressed young fellow.*

Tom Versus. [R.] Good morning—Miss—Miss—

Sil. [*Looks at him intently.*] What do you wish?

Tom. [R., *aside.*] By Jove! She's handsome. [*Aloud.*] I should like to know if a Mr. Kit Vandusen lives here. Miss—Miss—

Sil. Kit? that's my brother.

Tom. Your brother? [*Aside.*] I didn't know he had a sister, and yet I thought I knew all about him. [*Aloud.*] But 'twas ever thus. We imagine we are thoroughly posted about a man and yet his greatest recommendation [*bows*] remains unknown.

Sil. [L.., *curtseys.*] Oh, thank you.

Tom. For what?

Sil. [*Disconcerted.*] I thought you were paying me a compliment.

Tom. My dear Miss Vandusen, if your perfections were targets and my praises were arrows, they would fall far short of the mark.

Sil. Oh, thank you. Don't do it any more, please. That one hit. [*Crosses to* R.] I am quite unaccustomed to such flattery.

Tom. [L..] Indeed. Then they must keep you away from the gaze of impressionable man.

Sil. Well, I'm not secluded exactly; but I have to keep out of the way, 'till my aunt gets married.

Tom. [*Smiles.*] How old is your aunt?

Sil. Well, both of us together are fifty.

Tom. I see. Aunt old;—disappointed, lean, lank, sour and savage. You, young, fresh, beautiful, beloved by everybody. Tyrannical persecution. Immured from the world, but not for ever. Look up; hope. *He* will come. Radiant with love and hope. His bright eye flashing, his dark hair flowing. [*Running hand through his hair.*] His hair will be dark. Chestnut brown.

Sil. [*Laughing.*] Allow me to call my brother and tell him you are here. [*Exits,* C. R.]

Tom [*Looks after her.*] She's charming. Now that I begin to find Mr. Kit Vandusen the possessor of such a sister, I begin to take renewed interest in my mission. Let us prepare for the interview. My notes [*Takes out note-book and opens it.*] are full and explicit. I am first to touch lightly on the history of the heroic music teacher and the exemplary son. Then unfold the purpose of a mysterious benefactor—my friend and client, Miss Mary Forrest, who has heard their story and intends to make them happy. The lover shall not despair, the maiden shall not pine, the mother shall not die. A competence will be settled upon them—conditioned upon their immediate marriage. All complete. [*Shuts book and ruminates.*] I have found the exemplary son, the despairing lover, Mr. Kit Vandusen. I am to send him to Miss Mary Forrest. She will do the rest; reunite him to the music teacher, who has pined so long. I should do very little credit to my own penetration if I doubted for one moment it was Mary herself. She was a teacher of the pianoforte, which is the same as music, if you know how to play. Happy Kit. He will get half a million and his long-lost love.

2

Silena. My brother will be here immediately. Please take a seat. [*Points to sofa,* C.]

Tom. [C.] Will you? [*She sits* L., *then he does* C.] I hope you told him there was no hurry. An hour or two makes no difference, if you can stay. [*Rises and bows.*]

Sil. [L., *rises and bows.*] Oh, thank you. Kit can't imagine what you want with him.

Tom. I bring him some very agreeable and unlooked for intelligence.

Sil. Oh! is it a great secret?

Tom. It is.

Sil. Oh! are you a government official, or something?

Tom. No, I'm only a lawyer.

Sil. Oh! Do you dance?

Tom. Dance? It's not exacted by the rules of the Supreme Court as a qualification for the bar, but individually I do dance, and personally I like to.

Sil. [*Sitting on sofa, moves nearer to him.*] I'm so glad. I love dancing so much, and young dancing men are so scarce now-a-days.

Tom. Do you go to balls? Are you going to the Triton Masquerade, next week? They give it at the Hippodrome this year, you know.

Sil. Oh, I should love a masquerade. But 'till aunt's engaged I have to stay at home.

Tom. That's a poor prospect, to wait for the engagement of a maiden aunt of fifty.

Sil. [*Quickly.*] You forget that *I* am counted in the fifty.

Tom. [*Rises and bows.*] I could not forget you.

Sil. Thank you. [*Rises.*] But here's my brother. I must go. [*Seriously and bowing.*] I have been very much entertained.

Tom. The pleasure on my side has been ten-fold.

Sil. Oh, thank you. [*Going, aside.*] He's just splendid. [*Exits,* R. D.]

Tom. What an ingenuous little thing; says: "Thank you" for every compliment.

KIT *enters*, C. R.

Kit. [L.] You wish to see me?

Tom. [R., *aside.*] Fine-looking fellow. Mary has taste. [*Aloud.*] I come on a delicate errand—very delicate. Affairs of the heart, the domain of the affections, the uniting of kindred souls, are a little out of the common, as professional employment, but it's got to be done and I'm here to do it.

Kit. [*Crosses to* R., *looks at him, aside.*] It can't be possible.' Has mother actually set a matrimonial agent at work? [*To Tom.*] It's too absurd. My dear sir, my mother—

Tom. Don't say. a word, sir! Not necessary—it's all right. Your devotion to your mother, your unselfish sacrifice—I know all. I sympathize with you deeply.

Kit. [*Looks at him.*] Do you? [*Turns and aside.*] It's astounding—

Tom. [*Sits* C.] But to the point. I represent a young lady who has just come into a large fortune, which enables her to give full sway to the dictates of an emotional nature.

Kit. [*Sits* R. *of sofa.*] Well, sir—you represent this young lady?

Tom. Who requests the pleasure of a visit from you this afternoon at four o'clock.

Kit. And the address.

Tom. [*Giving card.*] She is stopping at present at my house with my mother, being herself an orphan.

Kit. An orphan.

Tom. Yes—the young lady—and a friend of our family from infancy. I am not permitted at present, for obvious reasons, to disclose her name. You will discover it from her own lips.

Kit. [*After considering card.*] I'm a little green in these matters. Am I required to say anything in particular when I see her, or wait for her to begin the conversation?

Tom. If you've got anything to say, I suppose you'll say it. I always do. [*Crosses to* R.]

Kit. [*Rises.*] Well, I'll come. And take the greatest pains to act the amiable, and secure *you* your commission. Good morning! [*Going up* C.] It's wonderful. [*Exits,* C. R.]

Tom. [*Watches him off, turns.*] I like the sister better.

MRS. VANDUSEN *enters,* R. D.

Mrs. Vandusen. Caroline said a person had called. [*Sees Tom.*] Ah! You wish—

Tom. [L.] My mission is ended, my dear madam. I have spoken to Mr. Vandusen.

Mrs. V. I am Mrs. Vandusen.

Tom. [*In admiration.*] The mother! [*Advances with outstretched hands, takes hers.*] Madam! I am most happy to make your acquaintance.

Mrs. V. [*Trying to free her hands.*] What do you say, sir?

Tom. [*Releasing her, folding his arms, exhorting her.*] Courage, poor mother. Courage, noble creature! [*Mrs. V. comes down, looking at him.*] It's a long lane that has no turning; even misfortune must have an end.

Mrs. V. My dear sir—

Tom. You have suffered. You have lost your husband. You will never get another.

Mrs. V. Sir!

Tom. I mean you will never want another. But you have a son—an heroic son, and a lovely daughter. [*Catches her hands.*] Cherish that daughter. She was the first to receive the dove bearing the olive branch in its beak. I was the dove, the olive branch is peace. Peace after all your sufferings. [*Hurriedly.*] I represent a wealthy heiress—Miss Mary Forrest. Now you can guess all. Courage, poor mother, courage! [*Shakes her hands, and at door.*] Courage! [*Exits, c.*]

Mrs. V. The man must be crazy. Miss Mary Forrest? I never even heard the name before, and he referred to my husband. I'll just call Christopher and ask him what it's all about. [*Takes Silena's letter from table.*] What's this? a letter to my daughter. Is it possible that innocent child corresponds behind my back? [*Runs over it.*] Piano teacher—Mary Forrest—the very name. [*Reads further.*] Why, here is my husband's own story related in this boarding school. Let me see about this. [*Reads.*] "Miss Forrest heard all the particulars from one of the chief actors in the drama, Silena Summers herself. She now declares it her resolution to bring the unhappy couple together. I have money, she says, it shall be the means of uniting those noble hearts. I will search for the devoted lover and son. I will—" [*Drops the letter.*] Everything is turning round in my head. This person going to find my husband and unite him to Silena Summers! Where is this wealthy lunatic? She must have sent the other insane person who was here just now. And he has seen Vandusen and spoken to him. Good heavens! His mysterious language, "You have lost your husband." Can it be possible they were secretly married? Oh, pshaw! [*Sits and holds her head.*] It's nonsense! there's some mistake, of course. But whatever it is, there's a mystery I must solve. [*Puts letter in her pocket and rises.*]

SILENA *running in,* C. L.

Silena. He's coming!

Mrs. V. [*Starting.*] Who's coming?

Sil. [*Mysteriously.*] Mr. Geagle!

Mrs. V. I can't see him. You stay here till I send your aunt down.

Sil. But suppose he commences to whisper?

Mrs. V. Don't hear anything he says. [*Sternly.*] You and I, Miss, have a little account to settle afterward.

Sil. [*Aside, and frightened, feeling in pocket.*] I left my letter on the desk.

Mrs. V. Deceitful girl!

Sil. [*Crying.*] Don't say that, mamma. Upon my honor, I would not conceal from you anything important.

Mrs. V. [*In tremulous tones, drawing her toward her.*] You ought to be a comfort to me. [*About to push her away, recalls the purpose and kisses her.*] Be a good, dear, little child! [*Exits, R. D., hurriedly, handkerchief to eyes.*]

Sil. [*Surprised.*] Mamma kissed me, like papa did. What *is* the matter with my parents to-day. I know they're out of humor on aunt's account. Why don't Mr. Geagle say what he wants—whether he wants to marry her or not. Suppose I ask him. I've a great mind to. He'd have to give *me* an answer one way or the other. [*Determined.*] I'll do it. I'll secure a husband for aunty, liberty for myself and a waltz with the dancing lawyer. [*Gets L.*]

GEAGLE *enters,* C. L., *a man about 50, neatly dressed, quite bald, save a narrow fringe of hair around the sides of his head. Extremely smiling and confidential in his address. Looks at Silena, smiles, lays his hat on chair,* R., *looks again and smiles. Unbuttons a long ulster, takes it off, folds it. Looks for a chair to put it on,* L. *Looks at her, smiles again, deposits coat* R., *then comes down, hat in hand, softly. Keeps hat behind him.*

Geagle. [*Whispers in her ear,* R.] Good morning! [*Nods, winks and smiles.*]

Sil. [*Takes his hand, leads him to* L. *corner, and in his ear.*] How do you find yourself to-day?

Geagle. [*Looks at her beamingly.*] Pretty well, but I don't sleep.

Sil. [*Leads him to* R. *corner, and as before.*] Why?

Geagle. [*Tapping his head.*] Buzzing in my head.

Sil. Lor'! what is it?

Geagle. I don't know. Perhaps it's because I have of late taken to deep philosophical inquiries. I discuss with myself: Who are you? Why are you here? What for? Why do you exist?

Sil. Well, what do you make of it?

Geagle. [*Looking around.*] Nothing—really nothing. Of course, I didn't come on the planet to collect curiosities. That affords employment for about one-eighth of one per cent. of my intellectual and physical faculties. Then what is the rest of me for? In the evening [*mysteriously*], when it grows dark and I'm all alone, and everybody is sitting at home with wives and children, I become depressed. I feel a want—a void—a vacuum—

Sil. [*Same, to* R.] You want a wife.

Geagle. My dear, it is only a short time since I have been able to accumulate capital enough to support a wife.

Sil. [L.] Then why don't you marry now?

Geagle. I would, but I've been having a race with Time. I've been piling up dollars and he's been piling up years.

Sil. That's nothing. All you have to do is to look out for some one who is not too young. Haven't you had your eye on somebody already?

Geagle. [*Seizing her hand.*] I wouldn't breathe it for the world.

Sil. But I've seen and I know.

Geagle. [*Same.*] I hope no one else noticed it.

Sil. No! No one but I.

Geagle. [*Stage* R. *and back.*] How clever the children are now-a-days.

Sil. So you do love Aunt Dosie? Eh?

Geagle. I don't know if it's love, not having had any experience.

Sil. Aunt Dosie is a mighty fine-looking woman.

Geagle. Is she? [*Crosses to* L.] ·I'm so near-sighted. At all events, she'd suit me better than a young girl. But I'm afraid of being refused. [*Close to her.*]

Sil. [R.] Why should she refuse you?

Geagle. [*Looking around cautiously.*] Because—I wear a wig!

Sil. [*Regarding his bald head.*] You wear a wig? [*Astonished, walks round him.*]

Geagle. I don't wonder you look astonished. It's made to imitate nature so perfectly that no one would suspect with the naked eye.

Sil. [*Getting* R. *of him.*] You amaze me. Do sit down. [*Takes his hat to put on the table, looks in it and draws the wig out of it, aside.*] He pulled it off with his hat. [*Replaces it and lays hat on table, then sits beside him.*] But why should your wig interfere with your success?

Geagle. [R.] Because it's a deception she doesn't dream of.

How could I tell her, and yet there should be no secrets between man and wife.

Sil. Then you'd marry her if she'd have you? [*He hesitates. Firmly.*] Yes or no?

Geagle. [*Determinedly.*] Yes! [*Rising, goes* L.] Well, what these children don't know now-a-days!

Sil. [*Calls,* L. D.] Aunt Dosie!

Geagle. [*Aside,* R.] I'm frightfully nervous. [*Feels pulse.*] I can't feel any pulse. And I've got a hot flush with a chill. I ought to have taken a pill before coming out, but I couldn't foresee the crisis coming so suddenly. If she says yes, I wonder if I must hug her or kiss her. I never did. I never could. I'll do it wrong. But she isn't a widow. She can't make any odious comparisons.

Sil. [*At door,* L.] Here she is. [*Clasps her hands.*] She looks beautiful.

Geagle. [R.] Now for it. [*Blows his nose and tries to get up an attitude.*]

DOSIE *enters,* L. D. *A maiden lady of fifty. Much overdressed and too youthfully painted. Hair in long braids with ribbons, but not too much of a caricature; quick, active and effusive.*

Dosie. [*To Silena, as she runs in.*] Did you call me, darling? [*Stops, bashfully, on seeing Geagle, then, placing her arm around Silena, a-la school-girl, comes down with her.*] How do you do, Mr. Geagle? [*Giggles with* SILENA, *hides her blushes in the latter's shoulders.*]

Geagle. [*Gasping for breath.*] Gug—gug—good morning. [*Aside.*] How dry my larynx is.

Sil. Aunt, dear, Mr. Geagle has something important to say to you.

Dosie. Me, darling? It's some little foolish, foolish thing, only fit for giddy girls. [*Smiles sweetly at Geagle.*]

Sil. You'll be giddy in a minute. Just sit down here. [*Places her in chair,* C. *Crosses to* R.]

Dosie. What does the child mean?

Sil. [*To Geagle, whom she takes by the hand and seats beside Dosie in another chair.*] And you sit just there.

Geagle. [*Aside to Silena.*] Don't go away.

Sil. [*Stands off to view them; to Geagle.*] Speak up, like a man.

Dosie. What is all this preparation for?

Geagle. My dear Miss Heffron—Theodosia, I believe we have both arrived at an age—

Dosie. At a what?

Geagle. At a—period—a period when we ought to think of —of—you know.

Dosie. [*Aside.*] It's come at last. [*Aloud.*] I don't know what you mean.

Geagle. I'm only fifty.

Dosie. Oh, years make no difference.

Geagle. Oh, yes, they do. I consider that, particularly in your case—[*Catches a warning gesture from* SIL.] I mean, in my case. Let us say *our* case.

Dosie. [*Decidedly.*] Never mind pursuing that subject. [*Simpering.*] What did you want with me?

Geagle. [*With a burst.*] To marry you. [*Jumps up.*] It's out. It's out. [*Blows his nose as he crosses, and takes stage* R.]

Dosie. [*With a cry.*] Oh, catch me! [*He props her up with one hand and fans her with a newspaper with the other, which he takes from his pocket. Recovering.*] You have so taken me by surprise. I never even thought of marriage.

Sil. [*Up stage,* R.] Oh, aunty! [GEAGLE *waves her off. She goes off,* C., *and afterwards peeps in,* C. R.]

Dosie. I had no idea of changing my mode of life. There is everything here to make a young thing like me happy. I was like a bird, joyous all the day long.

Geagle. Well, we'll be a pair of birds, and go off and flock together.

Dosie. [*Both sit.*] I can't decide upon the instant. I don't know you, Mr. Geagle.

Geagle. [R., *on seat.*] You've known me fifteen years.

Dosie. [*Sentimentally.*] It seems as if I had seen you but yesterday.

Geagle. Well, it *was* only last Saturday. Now to business. What am I to do, hope? Is it a bargain, or shall we call it off?

Dosie. I must consult my sister.

Geagle. Then I needn't go right off and drown myself, eh?

Dosie. Would I sit here if you were indifferent to me, dear Nicholas. [*Titters and drops her head on his shoulder.*]

Geagle. Dear Dosie. [*Takes her hand, then suddenly stops and draws back with a sigh, looking fixedly at her.*] I think it proper to call your attention to a little defect. [DOSIE *looks at herself and feels her toilette in alarm*] Oh, on my part. [DOSIE *relieved.*] A—a—fault—a deficiency.

Dosie. A fault, a deficiency?

Geagle. A big one.

Dosie. [*Soothingly.*] Can't you get rid of it?

Geagle. I do take it off sometimes, but I can't get rid of it altogether.

Dosie. How singular.

Geagle. Look at me, don't you observe something singular?

Dosie. You alarm me.

Geagle. The fact is, then—[*Places her on seat.*] I—I—wear—I wear—

Sil. [c., *who has been watching, holds up the wig.*] The fact is, aunty, he wears a wig.

Geagle. [*Starting away,* l.] What's that? [*Feels head.*] Why I didn't have it on at all. [*To Dosie.*] And you didn't refuse me, even though I went for you bald-headed. I am a happy man. Victory! [*Seizes* Dosie's *hands, and both go skipping over to sofa,* l., *and sit.*]

Dosie. Did you think I would have loved you the less on account of a wig.

Geagle. The danger is past. Now I can speak. We'll celebrate the festivity by a little wild dissipation. We'll go to the Triton masquerade, eh?

Sil. Me, too!

Geagle. You! of course. [*Motions her to retire.*]

Sil. [*Aside.*] They'll do. Won't pa be glad I've taken the business off his hands. [*Runs off,* c. r. Music. *Instantly re-appears, and runs to* l. *and off,* c. r.]

[Geagle *whispers in* Dosie's *ear. She puts her hands before her face, then whispers to him. He hides his face in his hands. She runs over to chair,* r. h. *He misses her, and looks under the sofa and behind it, then sees her sitting* r. *with handkerchief over her head. Steals over, lifts corner of handkerchief and says " Peek-a-boo."*]

Dosie. [*Running back to* l.] Nicky can't catch me. [Geagle *follows her. Both on sofa,* l. *He whispers in her ear. She shakes her head. He whispers again, holding up finger, as if asking for one kiss. She hesitates, finally throws her handkerchief around his neck, he getting on his knees before her, back to audience. She pulls his head forward to her and kisses him twice on top of the bald spot.*]

Mr. *and* Mrs. Vandusen *enter,* c., *with* Silena. *They all exclaim Bravo! Bravissimo.*

Geagle. [*Leading Dosie to Mrs. V.'s feet, and kneeling.*] Mother, your blessing! [*Back to audience.*]

Curtain.

ACT II.

SCENE.—*Handsome library, bookcase of miscellaneous books*, L. C., *and bookcase of law books*, R. C.   *Door of entrance*, C.   *Doors* L. *and* R., *table* R., *sofa behind it, chairs, etc.*   MUSIC.

JONAH, *an old clerk, in rusty black, is discovered arranging papers on table, has on white tie, pen behind ear, has habit of taking snuff.*   MARY FORREST *enters*, C. L.; *she is a young girl of* 21, *elegantly dressed.*

Mary.   [L.]   Is Mr. Versus in his office, Jonah?
Jonah.   Yes, Miss.   He's drawing some pleadings.
Mary.   Ask him if he will come to me as soon as he is disengaged.
Jon.   [*Going.   Crosses to* L.]   Yes, Miss.
Mary.   And, Jonah, I believe the callers for Mr. Versus are usually shown in here.   Will you attend particularly, this morning, to showing them to the outer room.
Jon.   Yes, Miss.
Mary.   [*Going to table*, R.]   That is all, thank you.
Jon.   [*Aside—going.*]   When a body comes into half a million, other bodies go to the outer room.   [*Exits*, L. D., *snuffling and shuffling.*]
' *Mary.*   By this time my letters and telegram must have reached the school, and Silena is reading them with more than surprise.   She will hear that I have found her Kit.   Poor heart!   She had given up all hope of happiness, and it was reserved for me to fill her with joy.   [*Rising.*]   What better use to make of riches!   When I feel her sobbing on my breast—when I see him clasp her hand—when they are married, and they shall be married—I shall have my reward.
Jon.   [*Shuffles in*, L. D.]   Mr. Versus coming, Miss.   He's in a hurry.

TOM VERSUS *enters*, L. D.

Tom.   [*To Jon.*]   Run off and post those letters, Jonah, and try to serve Boggs on your way back.   We must catch Boggs. [JON. *nods and exits.*]   Came as soon as I could.   [*Crosses to Mary.*] . Very busy this morning.   Most important divorce case. Lady in a great hurry.   [*Sits.*]   I sent you word I'd found your man.
Mary.   [*Sits* C.]   I want to ask you all about him.   You have really found Christopher Vandusen?

Tom. [*Sighs.*] Yes, alas!

Mary. What's the matter?

Tom. [*Sits next to her.*] What's the matter? I've found a rival, of course.

Mary. A rival? Do you love Selina Summers?

Tom. Why not? I presume that Selina Summers and you are one and the same person?

Mary. Don't talk nonsense. You are my lawyer, and a good one—extremely conscientious for a lawyer, and I want your advice.

Tom. [*Profoundly.*] State your case.

Mary. There is a young man, good-looking, clever, full of life, a little unsteady and flighty, yet brave and good, whom I have known since childhood. [Tom *looks at her.*] He never cared a snap for me all my life, until I came into a fortune, when he announces himself deeply attached to me. [*He rises, takes stage* R. H.] What do you advise? Shall I trust him? Come, answer like a sagacious and conscientious lawyer, consulted on a matter of business. [Tom *scratches his ear.*] Well?

Tom. [*Advancing to her.*] Well, my advice is, take him, if you don't find any one better.

Mary. [*Extending her hand to him.*] That is exactly what I think. So we'll let the matter rest there for the present.

Tom. [*Holding her hand.*] So you *are* Selina Summers?

Mary. [*Rising.*] You are mistaken. The proof is this telegram, I have sent two hours ago, to the true Silena Summers. [*Takes paper from pocket and hands it to Tom.*] Read it please.

Tom. [*Reads* R., *crosses to* L.] "To Miss Silena Summers, Music Teacher. Miss Bunker's Seminary for Young Ladies, Middleburg, Montgomery County, New York." It's a good thing they don't charge for the address. [*Reads.*] "Have found your Christopher. Come on by next train. He will be at my house. All is well. Remember the story you told me. Mary Forrest."

Mary. [*Rises.*] You believe in her existence now?

Tom. Well, I have a resource against the disappointment—the remembrance [*Enthusiastic.*] of a charming creature—by the way, the sister of your friend, Christopher—a delicious little innocent, who always says "thank you," when I pay her a compliment.

Mary. [*Surprised.*] Christopher has a sister?

Tom. A rosebud. Voice like a bell. Eyes like a gazelle. Altogether bright, and fresh, and beaming, like a May morning.

Mary. Did you intimate to Mr. Vandusen why he was requested to call here?

Tom. Oh, yes! I explained.

Mary. How did he take it?

Tom. Well, he didn't appear overjoyed.

Mary. He controlled his feelings?

Tom. [L.] Admirably, if he had any. Now, his mother, the widow, she was much more excited. But it struck me she was not altogether the helpless creature we supposed.

Mary. She is a most deserving person.

Tom. I don't think you'll find her a very thankful one. Do you know it occurred to me that these people may have got over the old fit—I mean the original affection. It must be a couple of years, at least, since it all happened. Christopher may have braced up and got another girl. [*Crosses to* R.]

Mary. Are men so fickle?

Tom. [R.] If I may judge by myself, there isn't the slightest dependence to be placed on any of them.

Mary. If they are all as honest there is some hope.

HANNAH, *servant maid, appears,* C. L.

Hannah. A gentleman, by the name of Mr. Vandusen, has called to see Mr. Versus.

Tom. [*Rising.*] I'll be there in a moment. [HANNAH *exits* C. L., *he looks at watch.*] I told him four o'clock. He's punctual.

Mary. [*Crosses to* R.] Please send him to me.

Tom. [*Going up.*] Don't forget you're to have me, if you don't find a better.

Mary. [R.] Suppose the "May morning" were to hear you?

Tom. Ah! the "May morning," what a pity most of them turn out November afternoons. I'll go and rattle off that divorce. [*Exits,* L. D.]

Mary. [*Sits on sofa,* C.] I am really curious to see Silena's lover.

KIT VANDUSEN *enters,* C., *shown in by* HANNAH, *who exits. He is carefully dressed. Does not perceive Mary at first.*

Kit. The lamb is led to the slaughter. I trust the victim is becomingly decorated for the sacrifice. [*Sees Mary.*] Madam!

Mary. [*Turns, recognizing him.*] He! who is this? [*Crosses to* L.]

Kit. [*Recognizing.*] You! [*Aside.*] It must be the same! That Sunday at the church. How is it possible?

Mary. [*Aside.*] It is he, and he belongs to another. I have brought them together. What a destiny is mine? [*Leans against table for support.*]

Kit. [*Hastens to her.*] You are ill; can I assist you? [*She drops in seat.*]

Mary. [*Motions him away coldly.*] Pray be seated.

Kit. I thought you were about to fall.

Mary. No—I—only sat down—energetically, that's all.

Kit. [*Aside.*] I'll marry her, of course that's all right. But how fortunate; mother might have proposed somebody else and then— [*Shudders.*]

Mary. Please take a seat.

Kit. [*Sits*, c.] I am at your service.

Mary. You are aware, I suppose, why you were sent for.

Kit. Certainly. I had a conversation with my mother, this morning.

Mary. Your mother seems to take more interest in the matter than you.

Kit. I confess I was indifferent, but now that I find you are the person—who—or the person which—

Mary. [L.] Let us talk of your affairs. You are willing to be married?

Kit. If *you* wish it—with the greatest pleasure.

Mary. How much of a dowry do you think a bride ought to bring?

Kit. [*Entreating.*] Don't let us talk of money. Let us speak of the time when we first met—when our souls, stirred by the solemn tones of the organ—sought expression for their feelings and spoke to each other through our glances.

Mary. [*Rising, excited.*] How can you talk in this strain to me! Do you forget that you are going to be married?

Kit. [*Rising and ardently seizes her hand.*] Yes; and I felt I ought, for that reason most of all, to show you that from the first moment our eyes met—

Mary. [*Crosses to* c.] Not a word more. Tell me what sum of money a bride ought—

Kit. Do you—can you—believe me capable of entertaining one sordid thought in your presence?

Mary. [*Agitated.*] The sum! The sum!

Kit. I refuse to discuss the topic. With me marriage is too sacred for the intrusion of a selfish thought.

HANNAH *appears*, c.

Mary. [*To her.*] What is it?

Hannah. Lady, miss. Says she is Mrs. Vandusen.

Kit. Mother! [*Aside.*] Come to see how I'm getting on.

Mary. [*To Kit.*] I'm exceedingly glad. She, at least, will discuss this matter in a practical way. ` [*To Han.*] Ask her to come in.

Kit. [*To Han.*] Wait a moment. [*To Mary.*] Allow me to withdraw. I don't wish to meet mother here. I'm not anxious to hear a practical discussion of the topic between you. I have some sense of shame in the matter.

Mary. [*Points* R.; *he crosses.*] You can step into that room, but do not leave until I speak with you again.

Kit. I will wait. [*Aside, going.*] Heavens, is there no youth—no love—even in her. [*Exits,* R. 1 E.]

Mary. [*To Han.*] Ask Mrs. Vandusen to enter. [HAN. *exits,* C.] Will Silena ever know the sacrifice I am making for her sake?

MRS. VANDUSEN *enters,* C. L., *shown in by* HANNAH, *who exits,* C. L.

·· *Mrs. Vandusen.* Have I the honor of addressing Miss Forrest?

Mary. [*Graciously.*] Mrs. Vandusen? I am delighted to see you. You are exceedingly welcome. [*They sit.*]

Mrs. V. You are extremely kind.

Mary. I should find it hard to be otherwise to one who had suffered so much—one who has the misfortune to be left a widow—

Mrs. V. [*Rising suddenly.*] Widow again!

Mary. [*Slightly amazed,* R.] I beg your pardon, but let us come to the point. I expect Silena Summers to-day.

Mrs. V. [*Smothered excitement.*] Do you, indeed.

Mary. I telegraphed for her this morning.

Mrs. V. [C., *aside.*] This is dreadful. [*Sits.*]

Mary. You don't appear to believe that I can effect the arrangement I propose.

Mrs. V. [*With burst.*] But what arrangement in heaven's name *do* you propose?

Mary. Well, to be practical, I intend to advance the necessary funds to remove all obstacles to her happiness. How much do you require?

Mrs. V. [*Controlling her voice with an effort.*] My dear young lady, will you first do me the favor to explain by what right you meddle in my affairs?

Mary. Silena is my friend.

Mrs. V. [*More forcible.*] By what authority do you dare imperil my legal and lawful claims upon Mr. Vandusen?

Mary. Why, don't you understand, I propose to put her in a position to claim him as her own.

Mrs. V. [*Rising, excitedly.*] And do you think, madam, that because you have come into a fortune, you have the right or the power to take away a woman's husband and the father of her children? Pray, don't forget, my dear young lady, that we have the police [MARY *rises in alarm*], and the laws and 'the courts to stop any such proceedings. [*Crosses to* R.]

Mary. Do you mean to say that he is married and has children. Christopher married!

Mrs. V. Don't you presume to call my husband by his Christian name.

Mary. Your husband? But he's dead, isn't he?

Mrs. V. This is too much. [*Shrieks and falls in chair.*]

Mary. [*Bewildered.*] There must be some mistake.

Mrs. V. [*Rising.*] There's no mistake. My husband was in love with Silena Summers—he gave her up for reasons that were sufficient and commendable—and this was twenty-five years ago.

Mary. Twenty-five years ago? Why, the Silena I mean is not twenty-five years old.

JONAH *enters*, C., *with envelope.*

Jonah. Telegram, miss. Just come. [*Hands it to* MARY, *who opens it—he goes, and aside.*] The fellows proposing by telegraph. Lord, what draft there is in half a million! [*Exits,* C.]

Mary. From Silena herself. Now we shall see. [*Reads.*] "Your message is quite a puzzle. I do not know any Christopher The story I related to you was that of my mother.— Silena." [*Aside.*] What have I been doing? How can I explain or apologize. [*To Mrs. V.*] You see, madam, it was an error, and all on my part.

Mrs. V. [*Pre-occupied with another idea.*] Yes—yes—I understand. But what is the name of this daughter—this— [*Points to telegram.*]

Mary. Silena Summers.

Mrs. V: Why, that was her mother's. How can it be hers! [*Crosses to* L.] *Who* was her father? [*In thrilling tone.*]

Mary. I don't know.

Mrs. V. She does not bear his name, because—because she has no father.

Mary. But she must—

Mrs. V. No *legal* father. It is shocking. [*Crosses to* R.]

Mary. Who can he be?

Mrs. V. [*Seizing her arm.*] I know him. I know him too well—and he shall know I know him. [*Up and down stage.*]

Mary. I hope that you will forgive *me*, that in following the promptings of a generous impulse, I have committed this folly. I regret having caused you unnecessary excitement. It will be a good lesson to me. I needed one. [*Crosses to* R.]

Mrs. V. [*Advancing to her.*] Don't apologize, my child, you have done me a great service. I am not angry with you. Dark deeds will come to light. My duty now is to sift this mystery to the depths. [*Wrings Mary's hand and going up* C., *aside.*] Oh, Christopher! Christopher! What have you done? [*Exits,* C. L.]

Mary. [*Solus.*] I do believe it's all Tom's fault. Hunting for a son he's found the father—or rather looking for the father he's brought me the son. [*Her face begins to brighten.*] But Christopher here—and *not* Silena's lover. I believe it's all for the best. He is free—and seemed to take a great interest in everything relating to me. Gracious me! How much better I feel now that I'm not doing anything benevolent. [*Pushes door open.*] Mr. Vandusen, we are alone. [*Comes down.*]

KIT *enters nervously,* R. D.

Kit. I suppose my mother entered into your views very promptly and thoroughly. I heard her talking quite forcibly.

Mary. [*Laughing.*] There was a misunderstanding on both sides.

Kit. Yes, I thought so from her tone.

Mary. But never mind, it has made us acquainted—oddly enough—but let's be thankful all the same.

Kit. Then we do not refer to the financial topic again.

Mary. [*Confused.*] Spare me. I deserve your ridicule. [*Sits down and indicates sofa to him.*] Won't you be seated. I believe there is nothing more to detain you.

Kit. [*Sitting.*] I'll go immediately. [*Pause.*] Do you mean to send me away now? [*Rises.*]

Mary. No—not at all. [*Rises embarrassed.*] Unless you wish [*Sits—he sits*] to chat about—

Kit. [*Drawing a little nearer to her.*] I should dearly love to chat about—

Mary. You left the school and the village very suddenly.

Kit. [*Quickly.*] Before I could manage to procure an introduction to you, I was summoned home to take a position that was offered—

Mary. I left suddenly, too, to take a new position for me—that of an heiress.

Kit. [*Advances, sits next to her.*] I congratulate you with all my heart, you are so good.

Mary. How do you know I am so good?

Kit. [*Moves closer.*] You remember the first time I saw you, it was in church—after all had gone—you knelt and prayed. I don't believe any one could be guilty of wearing a mask in such a place.

Mary. [*Coquettishly.*] Don't be too sure. I knew you were watching me.

Kit. You knew it—you felt it. [*Embarrassed.*] You have no family—no friends?

Mary. I am an orphan. [*Pause, both look at the floor.*]

Kit. [*Sighs.*] I suppose it is time for me to go.

Mary. If you have business.

Kit. Oh no! it's after four—the office is closed. Besides, I took a half holiday to-day, and I'm spending it with you.

Mary. [*Gives him her hand.*] I should like you to spend a *whole* holiday now and then with me.

MR. VANDUSEN *and* SILENA *appear,* C., *but seeing Kit and Mary, retreat,* C. L.

Kit. [*Overjoyed.*] All—if you'll let me. [*Knock outside.*] Did you hear a knock? [*Rises.*]

Mary. [*Rises.*] It's strange! Come in!

MR. VANDUSEN *and* SILENA *appear at door,* C., *and look in.*

Vandusen. I beg your pardon. We found the front door open. Somebody must have gone out in a hurry. We came to see Mr. Versus, the lawyer. [*Recognizes Kit.*] Why, my son, you here?

Silena. [*Crosses to* R. C., *recognizes Mary.*] Good gracious! there's Mary Forrest [*Running to her and embrace*], the " Beautiful." You know that's what we always called you. Our last teacher was the "Griffin," and the one before her was the "Cat."

Mary. [R., *embraces her heartily.*] Little Silena! I never knew your other name. [*They chat together vivaciously.*]

Van. [*Coming down to Kit.*] What are you doing here —with this young lady?

Kit. [*Drawing Van. down,* L.] Sh! Don't you remember mother's plans for my settlement in life?

Van. [*Vigorously.*] Which I detest.

Kit. I intend to meet her wishes fully.

Van. [*Sarcastically.*] What a good boy you are. But I won't have any such sacrifice. I'll set this matter right at

3

once. [*Turning to Mary.*] My dear young lady. [*She comes down.*]

Kit. [*Pulling his coat.*] Father, let me explain—

Van. [*Trying to release his coat tails.*] My dear young lady— Let me alone. [*To Kit.*]

Kit. [*Same business.*] But I tell you—

Van. [*Releasing himself.*] I do not wish to be told—I understand everything. [*To Mary.*] My dear—

Mary. [*Crosses to* R. C.] If you are looking for Mr. Versus, his office is the next room. He has kindly surrendered his library to me.

Van. [*Loftily.*] I was in search of that gentleman, but at present my business is with you.

Mary. With me?

Van. And I beg a private interview for a few moments.

Mary. With the greatest pleasure.

Kit. Father, you will certainly do me a very great injury.

Van. No, my boy. I'll prevent you doing yourself an injury.

Mary. [*To Kit.*] Will you consent to be banished to that little room again? [*Pointing* R.]

Kit. [*Crosses to her.*] I—

Mary. Are you afraid of what your father has to tell me?

Kit. [*Going to* R.] I am afraid of nothing. [*Aside.*] All's lost. [*Exits,* R. D.]

Van. [*Perceiving Sil., who has been watching with interest.*] Have you got another room we can put this child into?

Mary. If you like she can take your message to Mr. Versus.

Sil. [*Alarmed.*] Oh, I couldn't.

Van. The very thing. We have come to get a little marriage settlement drawn up. She knows all about the names, ages, and other particulars of the delinquents, and can give the lawyer all the points. The delinquents will follow within half an hour to sign.

Sil. [*Solemnly,* C.] Papa, do you really intend to send me to the lawyer?

Van. Certainly—he won't eat you.

Mary. [*Touching bell.*] We can call him.

Sil. But, papa, I don't know anything about marriage settlements.

Van. You made the match and you had better see it through. [SIL. *crosses to* C. *and up.*]

Tom *enters gaily,* L. D., *crosses to* R. C.

Tom. Once more unto the breach, dear friends. [*Stops, seeing*
Sil., aside.] The pretty sister!
Mary. [*Whispers to Tom.*] The May morning?
Tom. [*Same.*] You are an angel!
Sil. [*Who has been remonstrating with her father.*] Oh!
[*Vexed.*]
Van. You will have to, and that's an end of it.
Sil. I'll muddle it all up.
Van. [*Laughingly to Tom.*] My daughter seems to have
taken an extraordinary aversion to you.
Tom. [*Surprised.*] Indeed?
Sil. [*Pulling his sleeve.*] Papa!
Van. Now go, and don't be foolish.
Tom. [*Offering his arm.*] *I* should be terrified and reluctant,
my dear Miss Vandusen, for you are exceedingly dangerous to
my peace of mind.
Sil. Thank you! [*Exeunt,* L. D.]
Mary. Now we are alone. Mr. Vandusen, will you not be
seated?
Van. [*Loftily,* L.] Thank you! I shall be brief. What
I have to say may not be very agreeable, and will be much more
appropriately delivered standing.
Mary. [*Surprised.*] Indeed, sir. [*Walks away a few steps.*]
Van. Is it possible you do not blush to find yourself in
this situation? [*She turns, astounded.*] You are young—rich—
and, I suppose, respectable. Cannot you wait until your destiny
crowns your brow with the diadem of chaste and honorable
matrimony? What reason is there for you to anticipate it by a
resort to disreputable and speculative means—
Mary. [*Almost speechless.*] Sir! this is monstrous! You are
out of your senses!
Van. My son is a good boy, but energy is not his charac-
teristic. He has my disposition—heroic at the bottom; but the
heroism only rises at the strongest provocation.
Mary. Well, sir?
Van. His mother is differently constituted. She has ordered
him to provide for himself by a marriage with some wealthy
young person. I must do him the justice to say that at
first he resisted—because he loved another. But in the end I
find him here, ready to immolate himself in obedience to the ma-
ternal wishes. If I had not taken this opportunity to interfere,
he would have married you and sealed his misery.
Mary. [*Amazed and mastering her emotion, which has been*

perceptible during the whole of the foregoing.] Let me understand you. You say that your son came here in obedience to his mother's wishes. [*Crosses to* L.]

Van. To marry you, or rather your money. Ah! the crime of such a union. Those who wed should give heart for heart, not buy and sell them! To convince you let me tell you a story of real life.

Mary. [*Impatient.*] I beg you'll spare me that old story about Silena Summers. [*Crosses to* R.]

Van. [*Dazed.*] Eh?

Mary. [*Re-crosses to* L. *during speech, excitedly to herself.*] It was detestable to deceive me in that manner. Talking to me about the solemn tones of the organ—and the language of the soul—and all the while loving some one else and thinking of my money. [*Sits* L., *leans her head on her arms and sobs.*]

Van. [*Aside.*] I've been too abrupt. It was cruel. [*Aloud.*] Pray, don't grieve so, my dear. I was too severe. I beg your pardon. My only excuse is, I am a father who loves his children.

Mary. [*Rising and looking at him fiercely.*] *All* your children, sir?

Van. All? Of course, all! I've only got two.

Mary. [*Hysterical bitterness.*] Two? Ha! ha! ha! Two! Two!

Van. [*Non-plussed.*] Ha! ha! ha! [*Leans brow on finger in severe effort to remember if there were more.*]

Mary. [*At door,* R.] You are as false as the rest. With regard to your son, however, I will soon set your paternal mind at rest. [*Pushes door open and calls.*] Mr. Vandusen!

Enter KIT.

Kit. [*Aside.*] That tone bodes me no good.

Mary. Take your son. I have nothing more to do with him. [*Up to* c.]

Van. [*Aside to Kit,* c.] Come, my boy, and remain true to your secret affection.

Kit. [*Excited, aside.*] Father, you would not hear my explanations. This is the lady of whom I spoke.

Van. [*Amazed.*] The organ? the church? [*Turns and looks at Mary.*]

Mary. [*Suppressing her tears forcibly.*] Farewell, sir! We shall never see each other again. [*Exits,* c. R.]

Kit. [*Follows her to door,* c.] Mary! Miss Forrest! All is over. [*Comes down.*] And I was so happy! [*Crosses, agitated, by his father, on whom he turns suddenly.*] You have done very well. An excellent piece of business. [*Down* L.]

Van. [*Soothingly.*] It's all for the best.

Kit. [*Indignant, crosses to* R.] All for the best?

Van. [*Taking his arm.*] You may be happy yet.

Kit. [*Softer.*] You believe it?

Van. I'm· sure of it. There are dozens of girls every bit as nice.

Kit. [*Disengaging himself, paces to and fro; gets* R.] You are trifling with me.

Van. [*Soothing and detaining him, with both arms clasped around him.*] Very well, very well! You shall have this one. Don't despair. If you're true to her, you're sure of her. Explain and she'll forgive.· Come, let's talk it over soberly on our way home. [*Gets Kit's hat and his own.*] There is one thing, however, we ought to agree upon. [*Nervously.*]

Kit. What is that?

Van. To not mention what has taken place here to your mother. She always contends that when I undertake to rouse for action, I'm sure to do something foolish. We needn't furnish her with such convincing proof of the correctness of her opinion. [*Exeunt,* C. L.]

SILENA, *after slight pause, opens door,* L., *and peeps in.*

Silena. Why, where is papa? This is the room where I left him. I never saw such a lawyer. He .doesn't understand the least bit about law. Never asked me the names of aunt and her intended. Was very anxious to know mine. And he was so nervous. Kept continually mistaking my fingers for the pens, and grabbed them—so. If I could find papa. [*Going up.*]

TOM *enters,* L. D., *carrying several sheets of paper and pencil in . mouth.*

Tom. Oh! there you are.

Sil. [*Retreating up and getting* L.] I'm looking for papa.

Tom. [*At table.*] My notes of the contract are not finished. Will you be kind enough to proceed with your statement. [*Sits at table and spreads papers.*]

Sil. I will if you'll call in your clerk. For I won't stay with you alone. Not for anything.

Tom. And why, if you please?

Sil. Because you're so very nervous and make *grabs* for me.

Tom. [*Steps forward.*] You are so beautiful that you confuse me.

Sil. [*Starting from him.*] If you don't go about your business immediately, I shall leave the room.

Tom. It's all right. I am going about my business. Here's pencil and paper. Sit down. [*Makes room for her on the sofa beside himself.*]

Sil. [*Aside, deliberating.*] I won't sit opposite him. I tried that, and he looked right through my eyes. If I sit away off, he'll move right up to me. [*Looks round and sees law-books in case.*] I know what I'll do. [*Goes to case,* R., *twice, each time gets a pile of law-books and piles them in the middle of the sofa.*]

Tom. What are you doing with my law-books?

Sil. Are they law-books? So much the better. The law shall protect me. [*Sits down on the other side of books from him.*] Do you see? I am under the protection of the law. Now, go on with your questions.

Tom. [*Bending toward her.*] First! Have you ever thought of love?

Sil. [*Rising, decided.*] I am *going*.

Tom. [*Changing to business tone.*] Why, that's all right. How do you suppose you can instruct me to draw up a marriage contract, unless you know what you're about.

Sil. I *do* know what I'm about.

Tom. And *I* am trying to ascertain the fact.

S l. [*Sitting timidly.*] What do you want to know?

Tom. [*Ardently.*] Tell me, I implore you, have you ever loved?

Sil. [*Rising.*] Again?

Tom. [*Changing tone, and rapidly.*] I merely wished to show what questions are unnecessary. As matter of strict law you are not bound to answer. You understand? I see you do.

Sil. I don't!

Tom. Ah! Well, it's of no consequence. What's the name of the bride? [*Writing.*]

Sil. Miss Theodosia Heffron.

Tom. Bridegroom?

Sil. Mr. Nicholas Geagle.

Tom. [*Writing.*] The vast and varied experiences of human life furnish no more sublime spectacle than the union of two beings who love each other fervently. [SIL. *involuntarily takes one of the law-books, opens it, shuts it without reading it, transfers it to her left hand, with which she places it on her left side; this she does alternating with Tom several times.* TOM, *as if preoccupied, lays his pencil down and leans back; goes through the same operation with the books, alternating with Sil., both very slowly, he laying them aside on his right, and talking all the while as if to himself.*]

Tom. His soul yearns for her presence, her heart throbs at his approach.

Sil. [*To herself, looking at him.*] What a remarkable document he's getting up.

Tom. [*Same business.*] Love is the sunshine of human existence. It warms the heart, beautifies the world, and makes the universe teem with joy. It is the key to the mystic language of the soul, which we must possess in order to fitly communicate with the kindred being destined to share our lot.

Sil. [*Who has listened intently.*] How well he expresses himself. I can understand every word.

Tom. How wretched must that creature be who has never learned to love. Alone—uncomprehended, tortured by the dull round of petty cares, ignorant of a blessed recompense—living without knowing the true principle of existence, an uncultured flower, an unsought gem, an unrhymed line in the fragment we call life. Oh, how I should have mourned to have lived without loving—without having found an echo for the voice of my heart. [*Turns to her and in low tone.*] Silena! Do you understand me? When you pictured the man you felt you could love, and saw him in your dreams, was he so different from me, Silena?

Sil. [*Jumps up as if from a spell.*] The books are gone!

Tom. [*Seizing her hand.*] Silena! Answer me.

Sil. [*Wringing her hands.*] Oh, that contract, will it never be finished?

MARY *enters, c.*

Mary. You here yet, Silena? [TOM *begins to work furiously.*]

Sil. [*Running to her.*] I was waiting for papa. Please stay with me 'till he comes.

Mary. Why! you look frightened. [*To Tom.*] What does it mean?

Tom. [*Covering his head with papers*] I can't possibly imagine.

Sil. He draws up such strange contracts—it makes me grow hot and cold to listen.

Mary. That's it! is it? A poor child's heart fluttering near one of the traps set by the designing creature called man. Silena! believe nothing they tell you—they lie and deceive—all of them—this one not an hour ago proposed to my half million.

Tom. [*Angrily, rising.*] This is too bad of you.

Sil. [*Half pouting.*] I am mistaken in him. I never met him before this morning, when he gave me his card, and I took him for a talented, conscientious and accomplished young man

who wanted clients, and I intended to make papa give him all
his business. I would have done the same for any young lawyer,
or baker, or shoemaker. [*Half sobbing.*] But I am deceived.
I believe he's an old hand. I am sorry I took any interest in
him. [*Severely to Tom.*] For he's got nothing attractive about
him. Not a single recommendation. [*Exits sobbing,* c. l.]

Tom. [*Enraged, to Mary.*] That was exceedingly kind of you.

Mary. You are like all your sex, perfectly heartless without
apparently being conscious of the fact. From this time forth I
shall make it my duty to warn every girl I meet—to tear the
mask from their deceivers—to save them. [*Exits,* R. D.]

Tom. [*Calling after her.*] They don't want to be saved!
[*Comes down.*] I must say I feel exceedingly cheap. It's too
bad, just as I was beginning to feel that I was sincere—to mean
every word I was saying—honestly. I see how it will be. Back
to my old resolutions—shun the sex, fly marriage—rail at the
fool that yields. Just look at those books. All I've gained is
the job of putting them up again. [*Buttons his coat.*] I'll take
hold of that divorce now, and if I don't have the parties a
thousand miles apart in less than a week, I'm a Dutchman!
[*Exits,* L. D., *in passion.*]

JONAH *appears,* c.

Jonah. This way, mum; he brought his papers in here a little
while ago.

DOSIE *enters,* c., *elaborate street toilette.*

Dosie. We want Mr. Versus.

Jon. [*Looks around.*] Why! he isn't here!

Dosie. We can wait, thank you. [*Goes back to* c. *and calls
off.*] Nicholas, darling—this way! Come along!

Geagle. [*Outside.*] It's all very well to say come along, but
these confounded bundles—

Dosie. [*To Jon.*] Would you have any objection to assist
Mr. Geagle in with his bundles? We've been shopping and he
would bring everything himself. Ah! he's all right. [*Comes
down.*]

Jon. Yes, ma'am! He's doing famously.

GEAGLE *enters,* c., *arms full of bundles, carrying fancy parasol over
his head, open.*

Geagle. Where do we go now?

Dosie. [R.] Are you sure you haven't dropped anything?

Geagle. Just count 'em, will you. They kept slipping one after another, as if they were all alive. [*They slide off on floor.* DOSIE *flutters around him counting.*]

Geagle. Is the lawyer in?

Dosie. [*Continuing her count*] Thirteen, fourteen, fifteen. They're all right. What did you say? [*Sweetly.*]

Geagle. [*Sulkily.*] I asked if the lawyer was in.

Dosie. Oh! goodness knows. Sit down, darling—you look tired.

Geagle. Do I? That's remarkable! I *am* tired. [*Sits.*] Phew! [*Takes off his hat and polishes his head with his handkerchief.*] Do you know it's an awful relief not to have to wear that wig any more? I always felt like a perambulating tarradiddle while I had it on. But when you insisted I should wear it no longer—since I had won you without it—I felt as though I could do anything you asked me in return.

Dosie. It was a duck to go shopping with its lovey-dovey. What a heavenly day we've had. A girl needs so many things when she's going to get married. I believe I look a perfect fright. Am I too red, dear?

Geagle. [*Back towards her.*] I guess not.

Dosie. Oh! yes I am. [*Takes out pocket-glass and powderpuff, looks around at Jon.*] You can tell Mr. Versus we are here.

Jon. Yes, ma'am! [*Exits, shuffling.*]

Geagle. I'm rather glad the lawyer isn't in.

Dosie. [*Patting his chin.*] It was an old goosey, and now you must tell me what you've been worried about all day. Don't deny it. I saw you looking very, very serious several times. It wasn't the lobster salad, darling, was it?

Geagle. [*Gravely.*] No-o-o!

Dosie. Tell it's sweetheart. I know it *is* something.

Deagle. Well, the fact is we're going to that ball—

Dosie. Oh, Geagle! I've got my domino and my mask. We'll have a lovely time.

Geagle. Got your disguise?

Dosie. Yes! You've got yours?

Geagle. Yes—do you want to see it? [*Takes a false nose from his pocket.*] There, do you think any one will know me with that on?

Dosie. Is that all you are going to wear? [*He looks at her indignantly and then turns away.*] Well, now put it on, and let me see how it looks.

Geagle. No, I can't put it on now—somebody might come in.

Dosie.   Oh, now.   I want to see you in it.

Geagle.   There!   [*Puts nose on.*]

Dosie.   You shall dance the first quadrille with me.

Geagle.   I don't know the first quadrille.   I never danced a quadrille in all my life.

Dosie.   I can teach you in one lesson.   We'll try it now. Nobody will see us.

Geagle.   Oh, I'm afraid!   The lawyer might look in.

Dosie.   Just look at me.   [*Lifts skirts to show steps.*]   One, two, three—one, two, three—one, two, three.   [*Dances.*]

Geagle.   That seems easy enough.   [*Hitches up his trousers and tries it.*]   One, two, three—one, two, three—   [*Kicks his corn.*]   Oh!   It's no use, I can't manage anything but a horn-pipe, such as I used to see the sailors dance on the stage when I was a boy.

Dosie.   Well, let's try one now.

Geagle.   What, you can't dance a hornpipe?   [DOSIE *nods.*] What here?

Dosie.   Yes, nobody will see us.

Geagle.   No!   I'll stand around with the rest of the boys in a dress suit and look pretty.   I'll be a wall flower.

Dosie.   But just a little hornpipe now.   [GEAGLE, *after some persuasion, yields; they dance.* JONAH *enters at beginning and finally does some steps of his own up stage. After the dance, they drop on sofa exhausted.* JON. *has picked up all the books.*]

TOM *enters, L. D., at end of dance, L.*

Tom.   Well, sir.   What do you want?   [JON. *runs off,* L. D.]

Geagle.   [*Crosses to him.*]   We want to see the lawyer.

Tom.   [*Walks around him in amazement.*]   I'm the lawyer, I suppose.

Geagle.   [*Goes to him and whispers in his ear.*]   We came for the papers.

Tom.   [*Getting away from him.*]   What papers?

Geagle.   The contract!   The marriage settlement!   [TOM *looks him hard in the face, then pulls his false nose down and leaves it sticking on his chin.*]

Tom.   Are you the culprits that are going to be married?

Geagle.   [*With dignity crosses to* C.]   Yes, sir.   I am one, and this is the bride.

Tom.   I draw no more marriage settlements.   I make no more creatures wretched—you a grey-headed man—

Geagle.   Sir!

Tom.   [*Snatching his hat off.*]   Well, then a no-headed—I mean a bald headed man—

Dosie. Oh!

Tom. Whose placid countenance has been petrified by the blessings of a bachelor life. You— [*Steps forward.* GEAGLE *retreats behind Dosie.*] You give into the hands of one of those creatures called woman— [*Crosses to* C.]

Dosie. Who do you call woman?

Tom. The legal power to disturb your holy quietude of life, to distort the serene outlines of your face with anger, fright and fear; to rob you of means—money, friends, freedom—everything. You are standing on the brink of an abyss. Draw back before the fatal plunge. [*Crosses to* L.]

Dosie. He calls me an abyss. Help! Oh! [*Gives a shriek and drops in a heap, supported by* GEAGLE, *whose clasp has slipped up to her arm-pits.*]

Geagle. [*Indignantly.*] Look here—I say—see what you've done. [*To Dosie.*] Look up, my darling! Look up. [*Tries to lift her.*] This is a nice situation. [*Gives her a sudden jerk.*] It's no go. I can't lift her. [*To Dosie, with a shade less tenderness.*] Look up! [*To Tom.*] Young man, you've got this lady on your conscience. I wish you had her on your back. [*Jerks at Dosie savagely and with vigor.*] Look up! [*Gazes over into her face.*] I believe she's dead. Look up!

Tom. Dead? No fear of that. She won't die before she's married, nor afterwards.

Geagle. Look up! [*Jerks at Dosie.*] Look up! Heavens and earth! What shall I do with her? Look up? [JONAH *enters,* L. D., *and gets around to table,* R. DOSIE *at his next jerk suddenly straightens up with a shriek and* GEAGLE *throws her into Tom's arms and falls back exhausted against Jonah.* TOM *throws Dosie back and* JONAH *throws Geagle back.* DOSIE *totters to and falls in chair,* GEAGLE *same.*]

CURTAIN.

ACT III.

SCENE.—*Garden, decorated for the masquerade ball. Flags, banners, armorial insignia, exotics in tubs, etc. A centre-piece of plants with rustic seat around it.* MUSIC *distant; loud when no one on scene speaking. Scene opens with procession of maskers* R. *to* L. *and off.*

MR. VANDUSEN *discovered in evening dress, seated* C., *eating ice cream. When all are off speaks.*

Vandusen. If I were not so apprehensive as to what is coming, I'd enjoy myself exceedingly in this place. It's just twenty-five years since I've been out alone. How jolly it is—only I have an occasional hot and cold change when I remember my mysterious appointment for this evening. I'm trying to keep cool on a third plate of cream. I believe I'll try another.

WAITER *appears,* L.

Ah! waiter! Bring me another cream.
Waiter. [*Surprised, Dutch dialect.*] That's three.
Van. I suppose you have got another?
Waiter. Oh, yes, sir! But it's lucky you're taking yours now. When the rush commences—if every gent orders four plates—
Van. That's why I get all I can at present. I anticipate the rush.
Waiter [*Takes dish.*] All right, sir! [*Exits,* L.]
Van. [*Looks around uneasily.*] What can be the matter? [*Takes billet doux cautiously from his pocket and reads.*] "Dear Christopher:—I must see you once more before I die. I have something of the utmost importance to tell you. If you attach any value to the memories of the past, meet me at the masquerade to-night between 11 and 12 near the supper room. Your *Silena.*" [*Puts billet away.*] The poor thing must be very much changed. She forgets that we never were so intimate as to write each other as "Dear Christopher" or "Dear Silena." Well, it's twenty-five years ago and that explains. In my thoughts she was always

" Dear Silena." [*Looks around.*] It's extremely fortunate that my wife refused positively to come. I will take the occasion to talk seriously to Silena and insist on my family's account that she shall not address me in the future. She may think of me as much as she pleases—I have nothing to say against that. I think of her, but somewhat as I think of my youth, as something that I can never return to.

WAITER *enters,* L., *with cream.*

Waiter. Here you are, sir.
Van. [*Paying.*] And here's your money. [WAITER *about to exit.*]

TOM VERSUS *enters,* R. U. E., *in evening dress and stops waiter.*

Tom. Two orange ices in box five—
Waiter. Box five, sir? Yes, sir. [*Exits,* L.]
Tom. [R.] Ah! Mr. Vandusen. How do you do?
Van. [*Eating.*] Mr. Versus, I believe. You are an extraordinary attorney and counsellor-at-law to refuse to draw up marriage settlements.
Tom. Principle, my dear sir. As far as my experience goes, marriage is a short lane, with a wedding at one end and a divorce at the other. I cannot conscientiously assist people to pay so heavily for such a short excursion. [*Crosses to* L.] By the way, I suppose the happy pair are here this evening?
Van. Oh, certainly! With my daughter. They are in black dominoes.
Tom. Like everybody else—there are fifty black dominoes here to-night. [WAITER *crosses* L. *to* R. *with ice.*] How do you recognize your party?
Van. By the color of the bouquets in their collars, white and yellow roses. Miss Silena's is white and Miss Heffron's is yellow. [*Laughs and winks.*] Got yellow by lying so long on the shelf.

WAITER *enters,* R., *and crosses to* L., VAN. *speaks to him.*

I think I'll take another cream, waiter!
Waiter. What another! All right, sir!
Van. [*Imitating him.*] Yes, another! I feel a flush in the back yet. [*Exits after waiter,* L.]
Tom. Black domino with white roses. I shall find it. I'm a changed man since I met that girl. Can't rest, can't sleep— see her everywhere. Provoking, refusing, denying, delightful

May morning. I'll have to give in; have no defence against her charms, can't demur, don't object, and she takes me in execution—body, soul and senses. [*Exits*, R. U. E.]

GEAGLE *without*, L.

Geagle. I give you my word of honor. [*Enters*, L. U. E., *followed by* SERGEANT OF POLICE, *an extremely gentlemanly official.*] You are utterly mistaken; I did not intend the slightest impropriety, I assure you.

Sergeant. [L., *looking at him steadily.*] Several ladies in masks have complained about it. You go up to them as if you were about to whisper something and then kiss them on the ear.

Geagle. [*Indignantly.*] Kiss them on the ear? I assure you, Sergeant, I have not nursed the ruthless passion that would lead to violence of that description for a great number of years. My intentions were wholly mistaken. The facts are that the lady I came with forgot her fan and sent me home for it. I'm looking for her that's all. It's exceedingly hard to pick one black domino out of a thousand. I thought I had her several times, but on attempting to whisper the signal agreed on, "Your Nicholas is here," I found I had caught the wrong pig by the ear.

Serg. It sounds exceedingly flimsy, Nicholas, and I warn you for the last time, that if I hear another complaint your name will be taken and you will be ejected from the building—and don't you forget it. [*Exits*, R. 1 E.]

Geagle. [*Wiping his forehead.*] This is the first time I ever incurred the censure of the police. But I don't care—somehow I grow desperate. As the happy day approaches I feel miserable. For two days I've been dragged around the city like a—like—a— Well, the only creature who seemed to suffer in a like manner was a poodle—on a string—led by just such another foolish old— [*Checks himself, blows his nose.*] Well, a man can't make a supreme ass of himself but once in his lifetime, and I've done it. Havn't been near the club since I was engaged—am worked like a district messenger boy. We hardly got here when I was sent back for a fan she forgot. Walked all the way and I'm used up. [*Sits.*] It's a most extraordinary thing that a woman of her age should try to imitate the airs of a kitten. I don't like it—I don't want it. If I wanted a kitten I'd have gone in my back yard and looked on the fence for one. I selected a middle-aged person and she's playing *fifteen* on me.

TOM *strolls in again*, R. U. E.

Tom. How are you, Mr. Geagle?

Geagle [*Aside,* R.] Here's that monkey grinning at me again. [*Aloud.*] I'm pretty well!

Tom. Your bride is not dead yet, I suppose?

Geagle. No, sir! She got over it finely.

Tom. [*Looking off,* L.] I should say so—she's coming this way in uncommon spirits. [*Strolls* R. *in arbor.*]

Geagle. [*Aside.*] If she comes the kitten over me again, I'll try the *cat*—and we'll come to the scratch in no time.

DOSIE *enters with* SILENA, L. U. E., *each masked and with black dominoes—as they enter the* CAT *and* FROG *jump up and frighten them—then strut off arm in arm,* L. DOSIE *wears a bunch of yellow roses and* SIL. *white. They unmask as soon as they enter.* SIL. *stays at back and looks* L. *and* R. *as if in search of some one.*

Dosie. [*Perceiving Geagle, comes down vexed.*] Where have you been all the time, Nicholas?

Geagle. [*Sulkily,* L.] I've been looking for you half an hour.

Dosie. Did you get my fan?

Geagle. [*Draws it out of his pocket—done up in brown paper.*] Here it is.

Dosie. [*Unrolls it and throws paper away with disgust.*] I wish I had told you to bring my bottle of salts. I declare, I don't know what's coming to me, I forget so—but you can go for it now.

Geagle. [R.] Do you mean to say I'm to go back to the house for your salts again?

Dosie. [*Loftily.*] You hesitate?

Geagle. [*Pause.*] I'm tired to death. You are driving me like a cart horse. [*Sinks on seat,* C.]

Dosie. [*Instantly beginning to wheedle and patting his cheek.*] Excuse it's ducky darling—she's so excited. The happiness of being your wife makes her forget everything and everybody but you. You drive me into wandering, you naughty man. [*Geagle evidently begins to relent.*] You will go for your deary—deary—poor little bridy—pidy—and get the botty of salts—won't oo?

Geagle. [*Rising.*] If you talk like that, I don't mind going anywhere. Where is it? What's it like? Big bottle?

Dosie. No, little. You'll know it by the smell, darling—sweet.

Geagle. [*Going,* L.] I'll know it by the smell—all right. I'll be back as soon as I can. [*Aside—buttons coat.*] On my

way back, I'll stop in at the club and have a little hot spiced
Jamaica, I really need something to brace me up. [*Exits*, L. 1 E.]

TOM *enters rapidly, having perceived* SIL., *who puts on her mask
and comes down—he hovers about trying to speak to her.*

    Dosie.   Where can your father be, Silena?
    Silena.   [R.]   I don't know, aunty.
    Tom.   [*Coming down.*]   He's in the supper-room—I—if you'll
allow—
    Dosie.   [*Measures Tom with a withering look, and moves to* L.]
Come, child.   [*As she is about to exit, the* FROG, CAT *and* CLOWN
run on and frighten her.   SERGEANT *enters and arrests Clown and
Frog.*   CAT *has gone* R.   *He marches prisoners, crosses to* R.
CLOWN *escapes—he seizes Cat by the tail and lugs Cat and Frog
off,* R.   CLOWN *takes his hat and club and marches off,* L. 1 E.]
DOSIE *off.*]
    Tom.   [*Stopping Sil.*]   Beautiful lady, let me entreat a word
with you.
    Sil.   [*Assuming a false voice and angry tone.*]   Don't be so
familiar with me, sir.
    Tom.   Familiar?   Why, this is a masquerade—everything's
fair.
    Sil.   I forbid you to use such freedom with me.
    Tom.   Why do you treat me so coolly?
    Sil.   [*Sits* C.]   The millionaire young lady you proposed to
set me the example.
    Tom.   [*Sits* R. *of Sil.*]   You are unjust.   Miss Forrest had
some excuse.   I renounced her half million for your sake.   And
this is how you appreciate the sacrifice.
    Sil.   What assurance!   There never was such a brazen law-
yer before.
    Tom.   Do you always speak the truth?
    Sil.   Always.
    Tom.   Then tell me—didn't you come to this ball solely on
my account?
    Sil.   I never thought of you.   [*Hangs her head as he looks at
her.*]
    Tom.   You are indeed a miracle of truthfulness.   Such a
candid—honest—and frank girl is hard to find.
    Sil.   [*Tormented.*]   You are unbearable.   [*Rises.*]   I wish
you would go.
    Tom.   So you really want to have nothing to do with me?
    Sil.   I don't ever want to know you.
    Tom.   All right.   We shall see which sticks to his colors long-

est. For my part, from this moment, I intend to do all in my
power for you. I will go to your father and mother—to your
father then your mother—no—first to your mother and afterwards to your father [SIL. *gets impatient.*] and ask them for
your hand.

Sil. [*Angrily.*] Do you call that doing something for me.
[*Crosses to* R.] I wish you would leave off jesting.

Tom. You surprise me. Call marriage a jesting matter?
But never mind, my programme is laid out. First your brother
shall be made happy.

Sil. My brother?

Tom. Yes. I have a little plan that I intend to put in
operation immediately. Then you—

Sil. [*Mock seriousness.*] Do think of yourself a little.

Tom. I only covet the satisfaction of doing good. [*Laughs.*]
Au revoir! We shall meet—at the altar. [*Exits,* R.]

Sil. His defects are a certain obtrusiveness and persistence;
but apart from them I can't deny he is clever and funny—and
you can't get angry with him. Just as you begin to, he gets you
so interested that you want to know what he's got to say, and
then he comes out with more impudence and makes you mad,
and then begins to talk again; and so it goes on and on in such
a whirl that when he's gone its quite dull and stupid. Heigh
ho! he manages to have his own way, so that if he insists on
marrying me, I think he will. [*The* CAT, *close behind her,* R.,
meows in her ear. She turns in fright, L., *the* FROG *jumps at her.*
CLOWN *drives them both off,* R.]

DOSIE *enters unmasked,* L.

Dosie. Why didn't you come. I've had an ice. It was so
refreshing.

Sil. I wanted to rest here. [*Rises.*] You know, aunt, that
in spite of our masks, a great many people know us.

Dosie. Why, did you mean to remain unknown? I don't
think that's the object of a masquerade, at all.

Sil. But where's the mystification and the fun, then?

Dosie. Do you want to mystify anybody?

Sil. Certainly. And if you'll make an exchange with me, I
think I can.

Dosie. What exchange, my dear?

Sil. [*Takes off her roses.*] Take my white roses and give me
your yellow ones.

Dosie. With the greatest pleasure. [*In affected tone.*] The

4

perfume of this yellow rose is rather strong for my poor nerves. [*Exchanges bouquets with Sil.*]

Sil. [*Fastening hers on.*] Mr. Geagle will know you, anyway.

Dosie. Oh, I don't care for that. I shall enjoy myself flitting from flower to flower. He can have his fun flitting after me.

Sil. He will be very happy when you're married.

Dosie. He? Oh, certainly. But shall I be happy? I begin to fear he's too old for me. [*Sighs, crosses to L..*]

Sil. Somebody is coming. [*Both mask.*]

TOM *enters*, R., *running, crosses to* C., *stops, looks at both dresses, and then to Dosie, offering arm.*

Tom. I've found your brother, and I've found Mary. He's all right. And I've put my little plan in motion. Let's go and watch them make up. [DOSIE *throws an indignant glance at him and goes up—is met by Mephistofeles. She takes his arm and exits*, R. U. E.]

Sil. [*Putting her hand through his arm and holding him tightly while he looks after Dosie, and in assumed voice.*] Won't you stay with me? I've no one to talk to.

Tom. [*Aside.*] The aunt! Bah! [*Aloud.*] You must excuse me. I have something particular to say to your companion.

Sil. Do you know her?

Tom. I am happy to say I do.

Sil. You are in love with her?

Tom. It's natural I should be.

Sil. Why, she is a mere child!

Tom. Old age is no especial recommendation.

Sil. Do you mean that as a fling at me?

Tom. Geagle's looking for you. He'll be jealous. [*Crosses to* R.]

Sil. Never mind, I want to keep you away from my little niece. You'll be turning her head.

Tom. I wish I could.

Sil. Answer me—do you intend to marry her?

Tom. I suppose it'll have to come to that. As I would go through fire and water for your niece, I don't see why I shouldn't go through matrimony for her. [*Runs off*, R. 1 E.]

Sil. [*Clapping her hands.*] He loves me. [*Suddenly.*] But I'll tease him a little. He's very easily spoiled, and must be managed with great care, if I expect to train him for a husband. [*Exits in arbor*, L. 1 E.]

Music, *and* Masquers *enter for quadrille and nursery-rhymes, after which, when all are off,* Mary Forrest *enters,* R. U. E., *letter in hand, removes mask, looks hurriedly about, replaces mask as* Kit Vandusen *enters as if following her, with a letter in his hand. He looks at his letter then at her. She same. She wears a black domino.*]

Duet [*from Boccacio*].

> Strange request indeed, and unexpected,
> 'Yet methinks the author I've detected,
> Something tells my beating heart
> We are not far apart,
> I know we are
> On this—the spot selected.
> If I rudely shun the proffered meeting,
> She'll mistake my reasons for retreating;
> When in truth my only fear
> Is that the writer is not here.
> What can it be
> He wants with me?
> Here he adjures me
> To come – and assures me
> Something of weight
> He has to state.
> This puzzles me—what can it be?
> 'Tis he (she) what delight,
> I knew I was right,
> I'm in such a fright.
> Yes, 'tis he (she),
> Oh, yes, it is she (he).
> What delight your kindness to-night,
> How can I requite.
> I'm here as you see,
> What can he have to say, etc.

[*After the duet they sit back,* C.]

Kit. [R.] First, let me thank you for this opportunity of speaking with you alone.

Mary. I am perfectly willing to hear all you have to say.

Kit. A last interview was indispensable to us, whose friendship began so happily and ended so abruptly.

Mary. I am glad to hear you admit that it's at an end. It saves us much trouble.

Kit. Yes, it's at an end. All we have to do now is to look back. I was weak to yield to my mother's wishes. I sinned against my affections and my convictions. But I have the right to show you that a majority of the world would have approved my act. How many women have married so.

Mary. This is the difference in the cases. Women have often nothing but marriage to depend on. Men have themselves. [*Mask on.*]

GEAGLE *enters,* L. U. E., *coat collar turned up, pants turned up, rubber overshoes, too large for him, very smiling.*

Geagle. Back again! [*Smacks his lips.*] That hot spiced Jamaica really did me good. I took three of 'em. It was freezing cold, and now it's glowing. [*Sees Mary.*] There she is. I'll whisper the signal in her ear. [*Manœuvres around behind her. While doing so the* SERGEANT OF POLICE *enters,* L., *evidently following* GEAGLE, *watches him, his hands behind him.*]
Geagle. [*Bending down, whispers.*] Nicholas is here.
Mary. [*Starting up.*] What?
Kit. [*Rising and down* C.] What do you want?
Geagle. [*Alarmed.*] It's not Dosie!
Kit. What do you mean, sir. [*He and* MARY *go to seat,* C.]
Geagle. This is simply devilish. This makes half a dozen mistakes since I came in.
Sergeant. [*Advancing,* R.] Now I guess I'll stop your little game. [GEAGLE *turns, horrified.*] It won't work any longer. I spotted you myself, and I see what you're up to.
Geagle. [R. C., *after looking at him in a dazed manner, draws the flacon of salts from his pocket, removes stopper and mechanically takes a whiff. It staggers him.*] Ach! Ugh! Oh! [*Holds bottle out at arms length toward Serg.*]
Serg. [*Looks at bottle.*] What's all this? [*Takes a sniff that nearly lifts his head off.*] Ugh! Ach! Oh! Cork it! Cork it! [GEAGLE *corks it at arms length.*] That's a healthy drug to carry concealed on your person. Why it would blow the door off an iron safe. [*Stage,* R., *draws club.*]
Geagle. She said I'd know it by the smell. It's only smelling salts. The lady I'm engaged to forgot 'em, and sent me back.
Serg. [*Collars him.*] The old game again. It's T. T., old man, you'll just come with me to the office.
Geagle. [*Frightened.*] Are you going to run me in? [*To Kit.*] Kit, tell him I'm a respectable person.
Serg. [*To Kit.*] Do you know this party?
Kit. [*Advancing.*] Yes, he intends to become my uncle.
Serg. Then you must both come with me, if you want to get him out to-night.
Geagle. It's the first time I was ever collared by a policeman. I deserve it. A man of my age to get married. "Needles and pins, needles and pins, when a man marries his trouble begins."

Needles and pins! Egad! Handcuffs and jails. [*To Serg.*] You needn't hold me up by the collar-band. [SERG. *releases.*] I'll go anywhere. [*Turns down his collar and pants, and sees rubbers.*] These are not my rubbers. I must have changed with somebody by mistake. [*Hands them to Serg.*] Sergeant, these are not my rubbers, take them to the Club, will you. [*The* SERG. *threatens.*]

Kit. [*To Mary, aside.*] Wait for me, I entreat you. I shall be back immediately. Come, uncle. [*Takes his arm and hurries him off,* L. ·U. E., *impetuously,* SERG. *following rapidly.* MUSIC.]

Mary. [*Unmasking.*] No. I will not remain. It will end by my yielding against my own convictions. [*Looks round.*] This is my opportunity. I can regain the box. [*Exits,* R.]

DOSIE *enters,* R., *nervously, unmasked.*

Dosie. Nicholas does not return, and Mr. Versus pursues me like my shadow. He pours the most ardent proposals into my ear with a passion, an impulse, an eloquence that carry all before them. Oh, Geagle, Geagle, why did you leave your Dosie so long. There is danger, Geagle. [*Sits.*] I would like to find out if he knows who I am. It seems as if he did, though I refused to answer his entreaties. [*Sighs.*] If I had not accepted Geagle so precipitately. But I'm not married yet. It's not too late. [*Puts on mask.*]

KIT *re-enters,* L. U. E., *sees Dosie, mistakes her for Mary.*

Kit. Still here, my darling? [*Sits beside her.*] Thanks, a thousand thanks. This is a token that you forgive me. I so accept it. [*Seizes her hand.*]

Dosie. [*Aside.*] My nephew. [*Pulls her hand away.*]

Kit. Don't rob me of all hope.

MR. VANDUSEN *enters,* L. 1 E.

Kit. [*Rising.*] Father, join your prayers to mine. You were the innocent cause of my distress, help me to regain this angel.

Vandusen. [*Sitting on* R. *of her.*] My dear, it is your duty to pardon. My son loves you. Don't throw away an honest heart, or you may fare like my old sister-in-law, who got so ancient and was so afraid of dying an old maid, that she took up at last with a bald-headed bachelor. [DOSIE *bounces on seat.* KIT *and* VAN. *each take one of her hands*]

Kit. Oh, speak, dearest.

Van. Say you forgive.

Dosie. [*Jumping up and tearing off her .mask.*] Yes, I'll speak! I'll forgive you! Whom do you take me for?

Kit. [*Rising quickly.*] Aunt Dosie! I beg pardon. I thought it was Mary. [*Runs to* R.] Where has she gone? [*Exits,* R. 2 E.]

Dosie. [*Turns to Van., who looks at her puzzled.*] Your "old sister-in-law." Thank you. You will please to remember that I am the younger sister of your wife, and that in a few days I shall be a young bride. [*Replaces mask and exits skipping,* L. 1 E.]

Van. [*Solus.*] If she could poison me now, she'd do it. These confounded black dominoes look so like one another. [*Rising and looking at watch.*] The hour of the rendezvous, twelve o'clock, is past and Silena has not come. She has thought better of it. Concluded to stay at home and go to bed. Sensible woman. I think I'll try a piece of cake. If she's not here by the time I finish it, I'll go home and go to bed too. [*Exits,* L. 1 E.]

GEAGLE *and* SERGEANT *enter,* L. U. E.

Sergeant. I hope this warning will do you good. Don't try that manœuvre on again. We have strict orders to stamp out the least impropriety.

Geagle. I'm actually afraid now to stir a step in search of my future bride. The first time I think I've got her there'll be an impropriety, and you'll want to stamp me out.

Serg. You'd better come with me, then. I'll help you to look her up. [*Crosses to* R.]

Geagle. [*Takes his arm.*] You're an angel. A blue-coated and brass-buttoned angel. You ought to be Superintendent. Honest, now. Haven't you often thought so yourself?

Serg. Well, yes.

Geagle. [*Aside.*] I knew it! They all do.

Serg. But, I say, arn't you afraid of your friends seeing you walking with me?

Geagle. No. You are much superior to the average of the force. Besides, you haven't got me, I've got you. That makes all the difference. [*Exeunt,* R. 2 E. MUSIC.]

MRS. VANDUSEN *enters in black domino, mask in hand. Looks around cautiously.*

Mrs. Vandusen. It's dreadfully warm, and I'm so frightened. Will he keep the appointment I made in the letter. He received it. I know that, for I searched his pockets last night. The serpent, to sleep with that letter and never tell me. So far my suspicions are correct. He is capable of deceiving me. I shall not force his secret. I'll discover who that daughter is. Then let him beware. Some one is coming. [*Masks.*]

MR. VANDUSEN *enters,* L. 1 E., *in good humor, watch in hand.*

Vandusen. Time's up, and she won't come. Notwithstanding that last cake, I feel as light and happy—

Mrs. V. [*Lays her hand on his shoulder.*] Hist!

Van. [*Startled.*] Who's that? [*Turns.*] Here she is! [*Crosses to* R.]

Mrs. V. [*Assumed voice.*] Christoper! Dear Christopher!

Van. [*Aside.*] How her voice has changed! [*Aloud.*] Madam, permit me to correct you. I am not your "Dear Christopher," and I am willing to believe you are laboring under an hallucination.

Mrs. V. [*Aside.*] He seems very cool. [*Aloud.*] Oh! how you have changed, Christopher.

Van. Yes, I have grown old, and I hope you have learned how to do so. If not, I pity you from my heart.

Mrs. V. Have you forgotten the past?

Van. By no means. Let us sit down and talk about it. [*They sit,* C.] How have you been all the while?

Mrs. V. Well and ill—as fate used me. Often ill, very ill.

Van. I'm sorry for that.

Mrs. V. And these twenty-five years, in which we have not met, how have they passed with you?

Van. Better than I could have hoped. I did my duty; a reflection that consoled me when I thought once my heart would break.

Mrs. V. But you married?

Van. Yes.

Mrs. V. Have you been happy?

Van. Much more than I deserved.

Mrs. V. Indeed!

Van. Yes, I learned to respect and honor my wife, who was worthy of the most devoted love. Our children were born. I doated on them. I confess that you would have been forgotten, Silena, utterly forgotten, but that sometimes, in spite of myself, the—the—temper of my wife—her habit of command—forced me to recall your patient gentleness. [*Sighs.*] Ah, well! No one is perfect.

Mrs. V. [*Aside.*] What do I hear!

Van. [*Brightening.*] I hope you are not hurt at the frank avowal of my contentment?

Mrs. V. And you could be contented, knowing of the burden you left me to bear.

Van. [*Astonished.*] Burden! Our separation was your wish.

Mrs. V. But the consequences.

Van. What consequences?

Mrs. V. You forget our daughter.

Van. [*Jumping up.*] Our daughter?

Mrs. V. [*Wringing her hands.*] Oh, Christopher! Christopher! [*Buries her head in her hands.*]

Van. [*Aside at* L., *keenly*] This is some impostor, trying to blackmail. [*Aloud.*] Give me your arm, Silena.

Mrs. V. [*Rises and puts her arm in his. He draws it through and holds it securely.*] Where do you want to take me? Oh, you are squeezing me.

Van. I am afraid of losing you—come. [*Moves,* L.]

Mrs. V. But where to?

Van. To that little office just over there, where you see several police officers. They will be most happy to make your acquaintance, you impostor!

Mrs. V. Impostor!

Van. Yes! You are not Silena Summers—a woman as spotless, as stainless as snow, who joined the purity of womanhood to the talents of a man, and the courage of a hero. No—no, so just come with me.

Mrs. V. [*Struggling.*] Oh! sir! please let me go.

Van. [*Stopping.*] I will let you go on one condition. Take off your mask.

Mrs. V. Never!

Van. I intend to know with whom I have the pleasure of conversing, here or at the office.

Mrs. V. [*Threateningly.*] Don't pull me, sir, or I will cry fire. Do you want to create a disturbance?

Van. No, I only wish to know who you are.

Mrs. V. [*In frenzy.*] Let me go, or I'll do something dreadful!

Van. [*Struggling with her.*] You've done all the dreadful you're likely to do for a long time. If some one would come?

TOM *enters,* R.

My dear sir, come here.

Tom. [R.] What is it? What! trying to detain a lady against her will? You are going too far, even for a masquerade.

Mrs. V. [c.] Yes, that's what he's doing.

Van. This is no masquerade affair, my friend. [*Laughs.*] It's a masked battery I've taken by assault.

Tom. I don't understand.

Van. Will you get me an officer?

Tom. Is it possible!

Van. Or will you do me the favor to hold this person till I get one? The peace of my future life depends on my seeing her face. Hold her till I get back, and I'll do anything you ask.

Tom. Anything I ask?

Van. Yes. You have my word.

Tom. Hand her over.

Van. Take hold—so—so— [*Transfers the imprisoned arm to Tom.*] But hold tight, or she'll get away. Now, my interesting domino, we'll invoke the aid of the authorities to investigate you and your "daughter." [*Exits,* L.]

Mrs. V. [*To Tom.*] Oh, sir, I pray—I entreat you, let me go before he gets back.

Tom. Didn't you just hear me promise to do nothing of the kind?

Mrs. V. The peace of my future life depends upon it.

Tom. So does his. The peace of one future life is as good as the peace of another future life. So I think that I'd better leave things in *statu quo*.

Mrs. V. I'll scream. I'll faint.

Tom. Faint by all means. We'll see your face, then.

Mrs. V. You are a monster.

Tom. [*Struck.*] Your voice sounds very familiar. Have I ever done business for you?

Mrs. V. Oh! you know me very well.

Tom. Do I—what was it—shoplifting—blackmailing—perjury?

Mrs. V. What in Heaven's name do you take me for?

Tom. Not guilty, of course. Do you know that I begin to feel quite an interest—

Mrs. V. Give me some proof of it. Release me.

Tom. Show me your face—tell me everything, then, perhaps, I can do something.

Mrs. V. I consent, but in the strictest confidence. [*Unmasks.*]

Tom. [*Starts, and aside.*] The alleged widow! And engaged in an altercation with her alleged deceased husband.

Mrs. V. Well!

Tom. [*Aside.*] If I let her go, he'll be furious. If I don't, she'll be furious. Either way I make an enemy. And I want that alleged daughter. [*Aloud.*] What was the disturbance about?—perhaps—

Mrs. V. I cannot explain. But if my husband discovers me I am lost. He will never forgive my suspicion and my attempt to impose on him. Let me go and you may rely on my life-long gratitude. [MUSIC.]

Tom. Madam, I'll venture my happiness on a single word. I love your daughter.

Mrs. V. Let me go—and we'll see.

Tom. May I count on your assistance?

Mrs. V. You may—

Tom. [*Rapidly, and looking off,* C.] She is coming now. Will you leave me here with her—alone?

Mrs. V. [*Joyfully.*] With the greatest pleasure.

Tom. You are free.

Mrs. V. [*Masking.*] Was ever anything so fortunate. [*Hurries off,* R. 1 E.]

DOSIE *enters, mask in hand,* L.

Dosie. I cannot find Nicholas. Once I thought I saw him in a secluded corner drinking from a champagne bottle in company with a person in blue clothes; but it must have been fancy. [*Sees Tom and masks.*] That young man again.

Tom. [*Goes to her, clasps her waist and hand.*] My own! [*Brings her down.*] Don't avoid me. [*Overcomes her faint struggles.*] We must talk together earnestly and seriously, for our union is no longer a matter of doubt if you but consent.

Dosie. Heavens!

Tom. [*Leads her to seat,* C., *sit.*] Listen to me.

Dosie. [*Aside.*] Oh, Nicholas! where are you?

Tom. You must be mine.

Dosie. No! No!

Tom. Don't be frightened. I am not so bad. To offset the few faults we share in common, I have good nature, good temper, sincerity, devotion, tenderness, a loving heart and a thoroughly good disposition. These are little; but add passsion, the adoration I feel for you, and it is no unworthy homage I lay at your feet.

Dosie. [*Aside.*] He loves me. I am sure of it.

Tom. I have the best reasons for believing your family will not oppose our union. It is for you to whisper—to breathe—to look that *yes* I long for.

Dosie. Oh! spare me.

Tom. Your answer, dearest!

Dosie. Impossible.

Tom. You cannot speak. Then give me a token, a sign that you feel for me, that you pity me.

Dosie. [*Gives him her white rose.*] Here!

Tom. Emblem of your freshness and innocence!

Dosie. [*Suddenly, throws her arms around him.*] Oh!

Tom. My own—forever! [*Clasps her in his arms.*]

VANDUSEN, GEAGLE *and* SERGEANT OF POLICE *enter,*
L. U. E.

Vandusen. Just look how he has to hold her.

Geagle. [*Pretty tight.*] That's right, Blackstone, hold her tight. You don't get such a prize every day. What a thoroughly wicked-looking person she is even under that disguise.

Dosie. [*Aside and steps forward.*] Geagle here! What will he say? [*Falls back on seat.*]

Van. [*Alarmed*] Hold her!

Geagle. [*Springs at her.*] Would you? [*Turns up his cuffs.*]

Tom. [*To Van.*] Don't be alarmed. *This* lady will not run away.

Sergeant. [L., *to Van.*] What do you want me to do?

Van. I wish the lady to unmask. I must know who she is, because she has ventured to make an accusation as false as it is insulting.

Dosie. [*Astonished.*] I?

Tom. [*To Van.*] It was all a joke.

Van. [*Crosses to* C.] I don't take such jokes.

Geagle. [*Slaps Van.'s shoulder.*] I approve my friend Vandusen's course. We want the facts.

Van. [*Testily.*] Yes—yes—

Geagle. [*Irrepressible.*] If our friend, Vandusen, has been doing anything, we shall be glad to know it. If the lady—

Van. [*Same, trying to stop him.*] I've said all that.

Geagle. [*Same.*] We want the truth—the whole truth—that is to say, not too much truth—but just enough.

Tom. The lady is known to us all. I beg you to desist from your demand.

Van. [*Firmly.*] Let her take off her mask.

KIT *enters,* R., *and* SILENA, *mask in hand, appears,* L., *and listens.*

Tom. She shall not take it off. This lady is my affianced wife.

Silena. [*Aside*] His affianced? Good heavens!

Van. A subterfuge to shield her. You are not going to marry a person of that description?

Geagle. I don't know, he might.

Tom. Well, then, I declare solemnly in the presence of these witnesses [*pointing to Geagle and Kit*] that I intend to marry this lady. And I ask you to treat her with becoming respect.

Geagle. Show us her face and we'll show her respect.

Tom. You shall all see it. But I must beg you to dispense with the presence of this gentleman [*indicates Serg.*], as I don't perceive the necessity of announcing my engagement to the police department.

Van. I am satisfied. [*To Serg.*] You see I have gained my point without the need of troubling you.

Serg. [L.] So much the better. [*Bows to Dosie and exits,* L. U. E.]

Tom. [*Leads Dosie to Van.*] Show this gentleman your face. [*Aside to her.*] Fear nothing! [DOSIE *takes off her mask, so as to show only* Van. *her face,, then replaces it.*]

Van. [*Nearly speechless.*] Good gracious! And you say you propose to marry this lady?

Tom. I do, sir. And if you have any objections to make, I would remind you—

Van. Not the slightest. [*Grasping Tom's hand.*] I congratulate you. [*Shakes hands and goes up,* L.]

Tom. Thank you. [*To Dosie.*] Now show the witnesses, my darling. [DOSIE, *same business with Kit,* R.]

Kit. [*Astonished.*] What? Impossible! [*Goes up to Sil.*]

Tom. No, sir! Quite possible!

Dosie. [*Same business with Geagle,* L.] Forgive me! [*Aside to him.*] I can't marry you—I love him. You are free. [*Remasks.*]

Geagle. [*Thunderstruck.*] It can't be! [*Growing joyful, and to Tom.*] You don't mean it? Let me embrace you. [DOSIE *half turns to him.*] No, no! not you. You, Blackstone, you—my benefactor. [*Throws himself on Tom, who turns and flings him against Kit, who turns and throws him sitting on stairs,* R.]

Tom. I do not exactly comprehend your raptures, sir. But I accept your felicitations. [*Takes Dosie by the hand.*]

Sil. [*Approaching, indignantly.*] Accept mine also.

Tom. [*Staring at her, open-mouthed.*] Wha—what—

Sil. [*Tears yellow roses off and flings them at his feet.*] Base! False! Heartless! I hate—I despise you. [*Crosses to Van.,* L.]

Tom. Silena! [*Turns to Dosie.*] What have I got here? [DOSIE *tears off her mask.*]

Tom. [*With a cry.*] Ah!

Dosie. Thine forever! [*Throws herself on Tom. He struggles free, totters, and falls in Geagle's arms.*]

Geagle. [*With a shout of joy.*] Look up!

CURTAIN.

ACT IV.

SCENE.—*Same as first Act. The morning after the ball.* MUSIC. MR. VANDUSEN *discovered walking up and down.*

Vandusen. My wife, who stayed at home last night, has got a headache this morning. Her sister, who went to the ball, is as fresh as a daisy. That's very odd. As for myself, I'm all at sea. Mr. Thomas Versus, attorney-at-law, has played me false, that's certain. Dosie was not the female I gave into his custody. I've questioned her adroitly and she's perfectly innocent. All she thinks about is that young scamp. Now, what on earth possessed him,—with an aged mother at home—to steal Geagle's bride. He must be mad. There is one bright spot in the whole dark picture, though. Nicholas is happy. Ah! he's had a narrow escape. [*Front door bell.*] Callers so early?

CAROLINE *enters,* R. 1 E., *crosses to exit* C., *sees Van., stops, and familiarly.*

Caroline. Lor', sir! Is that you?

Van. [*Surprised.*] Yes, Caroline.

Car. Did you have a nice time at the ball, sir?

Van. I cannot complain.

Car. I guess they bothered you some, them ladies in masks. They always goes for an old gentleman as looks as if he was green.

Van. Indeed!

Car. [R.] Did you have any mysterious adventures?

Van. [*Stopping her as she is about to cross.*] What do you know about mysterious adventures?

Car. [*Confused, crosses to* L.] Oh, I know what they do at masquerades. [*Aside.*] I almost let out on Missus.

Van. Just explain a little more definitely what you mean.

Car. [*Going.*] Some one at the door, sir. I must be going. [*Aside, going.*] I'll keep out of his way the rest of the day. [*Exits,* C.*, on a run.*]

Van. What did she say about mysterious adventures? Can she be an accomplice of the unknown criminal?

CAROLINE *re-enters,* C. L.

Caroline. Please walk in, Miss.

MARY FORREST *enters,* C. L.

I'll see if Mrs. Vandusen can receive you. She's got a dreadful headache. [*To Van.*] Young lady to see Missus. [*Rapidly, and going,* R.]

Van. Caroline—

Car. [*Going.*] Yes, sir—directly! [*Aside.*] Not if I knows it. [*Exits,* R.]

Van. [*Taking out his glasses.*] Pray, be seated, madam.

Mary. [*Sits,* L.] Thank you.

Van. [*Looks at her.*] Why, bless my heart, Miss Forrest! [*Goes to her and insists on shaking hands with her.*] It does me good to see you. I was going to call on you this very day. Now, say that you forgive me, that you forgive my son, and that you are going to marry him, like an angel. [*She is about to speak.*] Now don't say a word if it isn't yes. But of course it's yes. You came to tell him—of course. That's why you are here. Why didn't I think of that.

Mary. If you thought a little more, Mr. Vandusen, you might remember that the girl has gone for your wife. I came to see her.

Van. She's in bed with a headache. Let me send for Kit; he'll do every bit as well.

Mary. [*Rising.*] In that case I can leave this letter for Mrs. Vandusen. Will you be kind enough to give it to her?

Van. [*Takes unsealed letter and turns it over.*] A letter. What's it about?

Mary. [*Smiles.*] No doubt, Mrs. Vandusen will tell you. It refers to a subject we discussed when she called on me.

Van. Called on you?

Mary. A short time ago.

Van. What for?

Mary. About Silena Summers. [*Crosses to* R.]

Van. [*Slowly dropping in chair and looking at her.*] I beg you'll sit down and discuss it with me for a few moments. I'm exceedingly interested in the topic.

Mary. [*Smiling, sits.*] As much so as your wife?

Van. [*Pre-occupied.*] As much so as my wife. There is a faint glimmering of light on the mystery of last night. [*To Mary.*] Did she talk about Silena's—

Mary. Silena's mother? Yes.

Van. No! Silena's daughter.

Mary. Silena is the daughter.

Van. [*Puzzled.*] Then who is the mother?

Mary. Oh, we know *that* well enough. The only question was who was her father?

Van. Ah!

Mary. You see there were two—

Van. Two fathers.

Mary. No, mothers. Silena, the daughter, and Silena, the mother. Both named Summers. That, of course, was mysterious.

Van. Of course, Silena's daughter ought to be Silena something else.

Mary. This gave Mrs. Vandusen a most uncomfortable idea. She began to fancy she knew the mysterious parent and that her own happiness was at stake.

Van. [*Smiles.*] It begins to dawn.

Mary. Her suspicions were so hurtful to Silena and her mother—and you—that I took the liberty of writing to my friend on the subject.

Van. Very proper.

Mary. There is her answer.

Van. From Silena?

Mary. The daughter.

Van. [*Rising, reads.*] "Your question was very natural. My real name is Silena Howard. Poor papa was stricken down in health and in fortune at the same moment, and when I saw myself forced to teach in order to support us all, it was at mother's suggestion I adopted her maiden name to spare papa, who is as proud as he is helpless, all the pain we could. That is my little romance."

Mary. You see?

Van. [*Folds letter, crosses to* R.] So, Silena married? That spoils my little romance. I wasn't constant to her image, exactly. But I—liked to fancy she was constant to mine.

Mary. [L.] The selfishness of the sex.

Van. Ah! we're a bad lot, Miss Forrest—all of us.

Mary. Not even excepting your son.

Van. [*Warmly.*] Now let me explain. He—

Mary. Give the letter to your wife as soon as possible. I'm quite sure it will cure her headache.

Van. So am I. [*Mysteriously.*] You don't know the extremities to which her jealousy led her. It's broad daylight now. The mysterious mask—the blackmailer! Who would have believed a woman of her years would have played such a prank. [*Changes his tone.*] Poor thing! how she must have suffered, though. [*Seizing Mary's hands.*] This news will make her happy. [*Pleading.*] Oh! if you'd only make Kit happy.

Mary. [*Disengaging.*] This is happiness enough for one day.

Van. I will call on you to-morrow with my wife. We will—

Mary. I leave the city to-day. [*Crosses to* R.]

Van. We'll call this afternoon. Where are you going?

Mary. I have not settled.

Van. Give me some message for Kit. What shall I say to him?

Mary. [*Moved.*] Tell him—that I said—good-bye! [*Hurries off,* C.]

Van. Obstinate little thing. The whole race of young people of to-day are like little pigs, with kinks in their heads as well as in their tails. [*Looks at letter and smiles.*] Oh, Georgiana! Georgiana! was it you? Have I got you? Won't I be revenged! won't I! We have been married twenty-five years, and to-day I am for the first time master of the situation. [*Rubs his hands and crosses.*]

CAROLINE *looks in,* R., *and, seeing him, darts across to* C. *to go out. She carries a bundle.*

Van. [*Calling sternly.*] Here, girl!

Caroline. [*Turning at* C.] Sir!

Van. Humph! What have you got in that bundle?

Car. This, sir? This—this is the Vienna bread the baker has just left for breakfast.

Van. By the way—what is your name?

Car. [*Flippantly.*] My name?—my name is Caroline.

Van. [*Solemnly.*] Well, then, Caroline, I want you to tell me the truth—as master of this house. Did anything extraordinary happen last night?

Car. [*Comes down.*] Last night? No, sir. Nothing at all.

Van. When did my wife go to bed?

Car. Eleven o'clock, sir.

Van. Was she sick then?

Car. Yes, sir. She had a headache.

Van. Is that the truth?

Car. I never tells nothing but the truth.

Van. Humph! And what have you in that bundle?

Car. This—this, sir—this is the Vienna bread that the baker—

Van. Humph! Yes. That will do.

Car. [*Flippantly.*] Can I go? [*Crosses to* c.]

Van. Yes! when your month is up.

Car. What do you mean, sir?

Van. That you leave in a month. I don't tolerate untruthful persons in my family.

Car. [*Excited, in loud tone.*] Sir! [*Drops bundle, domino rolls out.*] Oh, sir! Please, sir!

Van. Behave yourself! I have finished. In a month you go.

Car. I'll tell Mrs. Vandusen this very minute. [*Crosses to* R.]

Van. You may if you wish.

Car. This minute. I'll tell her everything. [*Going* R.]

Van. Hurry up, then! Hurry! Here! you'd better pick up your Vienna bread. [*She picks up domino, and exits* R. *door.*] My wife will be astonished! Well, it will do her good.

GEAGLE *enters, exceedingly gay in dress and manner—boisterously rushing to* Van. *and grasping his hand.*

Geagle. Ah! old boy, how are you? [R.]

Van. [*Surprised.*] Geagle, is that you?

Geagle. No! It's not I. It's somebody else. It's a transmogrification. Slept last night for the first time in twelve months. Woke up this morning twenty years younger. Look at me.

Van. New clothes?

Geagle. My wedding suit. Wear 'em to-day because it's the happiest day of my life.

Van. My dear fellow, you ought to wear weeds. A jilted bridegroom—

Geagle. I find it my natural element. Life has been a mystery to me for years. My eyes are opened. Nature smiles. Why? I have passed through great grief to great joy. I shall never be able to repay that young man! Never! [*Crosses to* L.]

Van. The lawyer?

Geagle. He has saved me. He is an exceedingly promising young fellow, isn't he?

Van. I'm afraid he has promised too much, this time.

Geagle. He got me out of *my* promise.

Van. You had better go and thank him.

Geagle. Oh! I shall, warmly! I want as a particular favor to stand up with him, only I'm afraid when I hear her give her-

5

self to somebody else for good, I'll swoon with joy. But I've sent him a token of my regard already.

Van. Indeed!

Geagle. A cartload of tokens, in fact. He! He! He! All the things I bought for *her.* I don't want 'em. He may have 'em. Good idea, eh?

Van. Excellent! I say, Nicholas. [*Takes his arm.*] What do you think will be the upshot of it all?

Geagle. Oh! He'll go on.

Van. No, no! He'll back out, somehow.

Geagle. I don't think so. They say he's wild with delight. Runs about singing and dancing. House upset—things upset. Says he wants to get married as soon as possible. [*Crosses to* R.]

Van. It's incredible!

Geagle. It is! But it's providential—for me. I've had my lesson. I'm done. I intend to find a nice young couple with a family, and adopt them.

Van. That's an idea. Sensible and generous. Have you got a family in view?

Geagle. Well, I've got the pieces—they're like a Chinese puzzle. I must get them together, and then I'll be all right. I'm after one of the pieces, now.

Van. Which one?

Geagle. The young man. Where's Kit?

Van. What do you want with Kit?

Geagle. To adopt him. I intend to make him a proposition: Business is business. I've got sixty thousand dollars. They shall be yours. You are to marry somebody you love, and let me bring up the children.

Van. Wonderful!

Geagle. [R.] Feasible, eh?

Van. Feasible and plausible. I've got the other piece of the puzzle.

Geagle. The girl?

Van. If you can put them together, you are the benefactor of two young hearts.

Geagle. I'll do it. When a man starts out to benefact his fellow-creatures, he frequently fails in the attempt, but when he starts out to benefit himself, it's wonderful how he succeeds. This is *my* happiness at stake. [*Buttons up his coat.*] I am going to do good to Geagle—and I guess I'll do it. [*Exits,* C.]

Van. He may manage. He's so happy, he'll infect every one. Nobody can stand such determined efforts to make them do what they want to. [*Strikes his forehead.*] But he don't know who she is, and I forgot to tell him. Of course he'll be back as soon as he remembers that he don't know.

CAROLINE *enters*, R., *impudently.*

Caroline. Missus was very much surprised when I told her what you said. She's getting up now. And she'll be right down to interview you.

Van. Don't forget—when your month is up.

Car. I don't care for what you say. [*Crosses to* L.] I'll go, if Mrs. Vanduseu says so, and she says I'm to stay. [*Exits*, C.]

Van. That's the extent of authority I've exercised for twenty-five years. The country demands a change.

SILENA *enters*, L. *door, her forehead tied up with handkerchief, groaning and leaning against wall.*

Van. [*Bringing her down.*] Why, my darling!

Silena. [*Piteous tone.*] Good morning, pa.

Van. Are you ill?

Sil. I feel miserable. I didn't sleep all night, and my head is so dizzy, and my heart so heavy. [*She speaks very feebly, her hand often wandering to her head.*]

Van. You've got the blues!

Sil. Perhaps. But that isn't what I came for.

Van. What do you want, my love?

Sil. You must go to Mr. Versus, right away.

Van. To Mr. Versus?

Sil. [*Nestling to him.*] Certainly—I'd go if I could, but I'm not able. The poor fellow is in a fearful state of embarrassment, on account of getting hold of the wrong one, last night. [*Hand to head.*]

Van. What wrong one?

Sil. He knew I was wearing a white rose in my black domino. So, to fool him, I changed flowers with Aunt, and that's the way he came to get hold of her.

Van. So he intended to get hold of you?

Sil. Certainly—he's in love with me.

Van. Very good, upon my word—a nice piece of news! Suppose your aunt won't let him off?

Sil. Oh, she must! [*Crosses to* R.]

Van. Yes, yes! But suppose he's in love with her.

Sil. Don't talk nonsense, papa.

Van. But I hear he's making preparatious for his wedding.

Sil. [*Insisting.*] With me!

Van. [*Positively.*] No! with her.

Sil. You don't know anything, papa. Oh, how my head aches! [*Throws herself on sofa*, L.]

Van. I know that you played him a very bad trick—made him look very foolish, besides leading him into what may prove a trap; and if he don't get even, somehow, he's not—

CAROLINE *at* C.

Caroline. Mr. Versus wants to see you, sir. [*Exits,* C.]
. *Van.* [*To Sil.*] I'll have him up now. Be reserved in your manner until we ascertain whether he wants you or your aunt. [*She sits down,* L.]
Sil. Oh! dear!

TOM VERSUS *enters,* C. L., *and down* R.

Tom. Ah! Good morning, brother-in-law. How do you do this morning? [VAN., *speechless, turns a glance of commiseration on Sil.*]
Tom. [*Crosses to* C., *looks at Sil. and approaches her.*] Ah! Did our little niece sleep well after the ball?
Sil. [*Bursts into tears and turns her back to him.*]
Tom. [*After looking at her turns to Van. and in declamatory tone.*] And *she*—the goddess of my dreams—has *she* risen from her slumbers?
Van. [*Looks at him open-mouthed, aside.*] He's a fool. [*Aloud to Tom.*] If you mean my sister-in-law—she's been up this two hours.
Tom. Oh, lead me to her.
Van. You want to see her?
Tom. I grudge every second that separates me from my love. [SIL. *cries loudly.*]
Van. [*Pats him on shoulder.*] Don't you cry, sonny. I'll have her here right away for you. [*Goes* L. *and aside.*] He's having his revenge. [*Exits,* L. D. SIL. *looks after her father, then goes to* C. *seat and sits, back to Tom.*]
Tom. [*Leaning against mantel, looks at her a moment.*] Well, Cupid!
Sil. Whom do you call Cupid, sir?
Tom. What are you doing with that band over your eyes?
Sil. [*Tearing it off.*] I've got a headache.
Tom. [*To himself aloud.*] Oh, that she were here!
Sil. [*Goes to him.*] You must not quite take me for a fool, Mr. Versus.
Tom. [*Astonished.*] What do you mean?
Sil. A person can be in love and not act as silly as you do.
Tom. As I do?

Sil. Yes—and I tell you—you don't love Aunt Dosie one bit.

Tom. Not love my bride?

Sil. Ugh! She's your bride because you thought she was somebody else.

Tom. You astonish me.

Sil. [L.] I know everything. I'm sure I ought to if anybody does, for I got up the foolish trick to change the roses. [*Beginning to cry.*] And I never would in this world if I'd known what would happen. Oh! Mr. Versus! Oh! Tom! What *are* we going to do about it?

Tom. So you arranged the plan by which I gained Miss Dosie. Accept my warmest thanks. [*Crosses to* R.]

Sil. [*In a rage.*] You are a detestable man—but one thing I vow: no matter who asks me, never! never! to go to a masked ball again. [*Goes up* L., *crying.*]

MR. VANDUSEN *enters*, R., *leading* DOSIE *by the hand.*

Tom. [*Opens his arms a la Claude Melnotte.*] My love! my sun! my star! my Dosie. [DOSIE *with a shriek rushes to his embrace, and is folded in his arms. Tableau.*]

Tom. My own!

Van. [*Stepping up and tapping Tom on shoulder.*] I guess I'd better go, as I'm only in the way. If you want me I'll be in there. [*Points to* R. *and exits*, C. *door.*]

Sil. [*Comes in front of them and savagely.*] And I guess I'd better go, since Aunt Dosie doesn't know any better than to go on with such actions before a child. If anybody wants *me*, I'm in here. [*Exits*, R. D.]

Dosie. How they envy me. [*About to throw her arms around his neck, he catches both.*]

Tom. Now let's sit down and talk sensibly.

Dosie. [*A little taken aback.*] Yes! [TOM *pushes sofa forward; they sit.*]

Tom. [R.] Now listen to me.

Dosie. Speak! Do with me as you please. Mould me to your will.

Tom. First we'll get married.

Dosie. Yes!

Tom. Then we leave the city.

Dosie. For a wedding tour?

Tom. No, for good. I've disposed of everything belonging to me.

Dosie. What for?

Tom. Above all, because the world will talk. This is no

place for us. You were the betrothed of Geagle. Now you are mine.

Dosie. I don't care what people say. [*Rises.*]

Tom. I will defend you with my life, for I love you. [*She is about to embrace him, he catches her hands and prevents her.*] I am jealous of that love. My angel, let them utter one breath of slander and they die. [*Crosses to* L.] Do you want me to fill the city with tombstones?

Dosie. [*Crosses to* R., *aside.*] How he loves me. [*Aloud.*] Be it as you will, we will go hand in hand.

Tom. [L.] To the end of the world—literally—for I have chosen my destination. We sail Saturday. I write for passports to-day. Give me your figures.

Dosie. [R.] My figures?

Tom. Your dates—born so and so—

Dosic. [*Rising.*] Nonsense!

Tom. [*Rising.*] Nonsense?

Dosie. I'll look in the book—it's down, of course. I don't know who put it, and I doubt if they knew.

Tom. [*With ardor.*] Send it to me—and I'll send thee—

Dosie. [*Same.*] What, darling?

Tom. [*Changing tone.*] A few necessary articles for our journey. [*Changing back.*] You'll not refuse them?

Dosie. I cannot!

Tom. [*Changing.*] With full instructions. [*Changing.*] For we must wander far, my love. [*Changing.*] And you must know what's before you. [*Changing.*] And now farewell, my sweet. [*Draws her to him.*] One kiss— [*Pushes her slowly back.*] No—no—it is too much. I must not take advantage of your youth and weakness. [*Sighs and rushes off,* C. R. *Meets* VAN. *at door, takes his arm and hurries him off,* C. R.]

Dosie. How he controls himself. What character, what firmness—and he loves me to delirium. [*Sinks in chair.*] What could have possessed him to go where we have to get passports? It's ridiculous to ask it [*Rising*], and I promised him to send the book. [*Goes to desk, unlocks it and takes out small 12mo volume, thick, and in old binding, opens it carefully.*] There it is. I never saw such ink for getting blacker and blacker every year. [*Looks around, whispers.*] There's a fatality about it. First of June, eighteen hundred and thirty— [*Shuts book suddenly and gasps, looks around, reopens it and looks again.*] 1830. I could make that three a five, but the whole date is written out in letters too. [*Angrily.*] But I won't have such a thing in existence. I won't. [*Sees inkstand in desk, suddenly seizes it and pours it on page.*] Now it's all gone—accidentally, of course. [*Calling.*]

Caroline! Caroline! come here, I've spilled the ink! Bring something to wipe it up! Caroline! Quick.

CAROLINE *enters,* C., MR. VANDUSEN R., SILENA L.

Together. {
   Caroline. What is it, ma'am?
   Vandusen. Who cried out?
   Silena. [*Looks over her shoulder.*] Oh, Aunt! what is it?

Dosie. Look what I've done. Spilled the ink bottle all over the book.

Car. [*On her L.*] Is it fresh? Oh, we'll soon have that all right! [*Seizes the book and darts out,* C., *holding it at arm's length.*]

Sil. How came you to have it open at the family register, aunty?

Dosie. I had just opened the book.

Sil. [*Mischievously.*] And the ink 'bottle flew over and blotted out all the dates, your birth among the rest.

Van. Very curious coincidence.

Dosie. What do you wish to insinuate, brother-in-law?

Van. That you were the accomplice of the ink bottle.

Dosie. [*Crosses to L.*] Wait until I have a strong arm to defend me.

Car. [*Brings back page clean.*] Here you are, Miss, clean as a whistle. The bleaching powder does it while the ink's fresh. You can read it like print now. Born the first of June, eighteen hundred and thirty—

Dosie. [*Tearing book from her.*] Girl! go about your business. [*Exits,* R. *door,* CAR. *gets* L. *corner, pretending to cry.* VAN. *laughs.*]

Sil. [*Wringing her hands.*] Eighteen hundred and thirty—that's old enough to be his mother. [*Exits,* R.]

Car. [*Weeping.*] I did all for the best.

Van. [*Kindly.*] You did very well—I am very pleased. You can remain when your month is up.

Car. [*Softened and low, after looking at him.*] Thank you, sir. [*Exits* C., *with her apron to her eyes.*]

Van. [*Goes to table.*] A great waste of ink, but enough left to write a note to Kit's sweetheart. That idiot, Geagle, won't find her. [*Writes.*] "My Dear Miss Forrest. I am sorry to say that I cannot deliver your farewell message to my son for the reason that—" [*Continues to write a line more and address the envelope, after he is interrupted by*

GEAGLE, *outside, shouting,* C. L.

Geagle. In yet—I'll find him. [*He bounces in—in a great heat, looks around—sees Van, rushes to him—drags him out of his chair, and stands on tip-toe to whisper in his ear.*]

Van. [*Having heard him.*] My very thought. Look here. [*Hands letter.* GEAGLE *opens it, reads, cries aloud for joy.*]

Geagle. What! Glorious!

Van. It'll do.

Geagle. I'll bring her—whoop! [*Seizes Van. and both waltz around to a lively air which they shout.*]

MRS. VANDUSEN *appears,* R. 1 E., *and stops astonished.* GEAGLE *releases Van., seizes his hat and rushes out, C. L., with letter.* VAN. *leans against sofa, laughing quietly.*

Mrs. Vandusen. [*A little faltering, but trying to assume her former command.*] You are exceedingly gay, Mr. Vandusen!

Van. [*Quite self-possessed. Fanning himself.*] Oh, no—glad to see you up, my dear.

Mrs. V. Caroline has a very curious story to tell me.

Van. It's nothing to the story she told me. I discharged her for it on the spot. I cannot tolerate lying.

Mrs. V. [*Amazed.*] Mr. Vandusen!

Van. Lying, my dear. She tried to deceive me about your absence last evening. She said you had not been out of the house.

Mrs. V. [*Frightened and half inarticulate.*] I was—I w—was—

Van. Of course you were out, and the unprincipled creature thought I knew nothing about it. Had the audacity, in fact, to suppose that you kept any secrets from me. It was an insult to me and a worse one to you. I acted on the impulse I felt as your husband and the father of your children, and I dismissed her.

Mrs. V. [*Stammering.*] Perhaps she thought—

Van. [*Interrupting.*] She thought you went to the masquerade to watch me—to play a part and to surprise the unworthy secret *I* was supposed to cherish.

Mrs. V. [*Going to him with clasped hands.*] Christopher!

Van. [*Still going on.*] She didn't know that I would have been the first to reveal everything to my wife, as well as the last to deceive her. She did not know that I carried [*Taking Mary's letter out*] a proof that I longed for an opportunity to show you. [*Gives her the letter, which she opens and reads, crosses to* R.]

Mrs. V. [*Having read.*] What must you think of *me !*

Van. So, of course, I had to punish her promptly and severely. But she has since given unmistakable proof that she is sorry for her fault, and if you ask me to forgive her, I shall do it gladly. For we will have but one thought and one will.

Mrs. V. [*Overpowered.*] I have done wrong, and you are heaping coals of fire on my head. Pardon me, my dear husband ! [*Puts her arms round his neck.*]

Van. Do you forgive her, too?

CAROLINE enters, C.

Caroline. If you please— [*Stops.* MRS. V. *about to withdraw from Van.'s arms, he detains her.*]

Van. [*To Mrs. V.*] Stay a moment, I want her to see there is no quarrel—no scandal—in this house. [*Releases her.*] There, she has seen enough. [*To Car.*] What is it?

Car. If you please, sir, here's a big box come for Miss Dosie from Mr. Versus.

Van. Bring it in, and then go and tell the lady.

Car. This way ! My sakes, it's a whopper !

Two PORTERS enter with big chest.

Porter. See here, how much further have we got to take this?

Car. Put it right down there.

Porter. This is extry. Ain't included in the express charges.

Car. Oh, ain't it? Well, you'd better go and get yer extry outer them as sent yer. [*Shows Porters off,* C., *and exits,* R. 1 E.]

Mrs. V. A box from Mr. Versus—for Dosie. Why, I thought that he and Silena—

Van. Never mind; let him do as he likes—he knows what he's about.

DOSIE enters, R.

Dosie. Where is it? [*Sees Mrs. V.—runs and kisses her.*] Oh, sister, you don't know how happy I am !

Mrs. V. [*Coldly.*] I don't know anything at all, it seems. What has become of Mr. Geagle?

Dosie. [*Unfastening chest.*] Mr. Geagle is too sensible, at his time of life, to take a young wife.

Mrs. V. I should have thought *you* were too sensible, at your time of life, to let a young man make a fool of you.

Dosie. We'll see who's made a fool of. [*Opens chest.*] Why it's full of all sorts of things. [*Takes out a box.*] What this — a revolver? [*Takes it out.*]

Van. A very sensible present.

Dosie. For a bride?

Van. For a bride who has to shoot tigers in self-defence.

Dosie. Shoot tigers—where?

Van. Where you are going.

Dosie. [*Takes a bottle and reads label.*] Poison!

Van. Poison. To take in order to escape a more painful death.

Dosie. I wish you would explain and not joke. Do you know anything about all this?

Van. I know everything about it.

Dosie. [*Draws out hammock.*] A hammock! [*Spreads it out.*]

Van. Your bed.

Dosie. And this?

Van. Your blanket. You won't need any warmer bedclothes. [DOSIE *draws out a pair of Turkish trowsers, holds them up and shrieks.*]

Van. Your traveling suit. You are especially desired to begin wearing them immediately to get used to the sensation.

Dosie. What is the meaning of all this nonsense?

Van. My dear sister-in-law, you are going to Africa on an exploring expedition to extend the discoveries of Stanley. Mr. Versus not only intends to explore the vicinity of Ubjibbeloola, but to settle among the natives and convert them. He will probably be made king. You, of course, will be queen.

Dosie. [*Irritated.*] It's a very poor joke.

Van. It would be if it were a joke. But his plans, although spiced with the adventurous, are exceedingly practical. You will conform to the customs of the country. As queen, you will be at the head of an extensive harem, or seraglio. You will find thirty-five female dresses of all sizes in the bottom of the chest.

Dosie. [*Slapping the things back into the trunk.*] I begin to think you have taken leave of your senses.

Van. [*Sighs.*] Poor Versus has taken leave of his—his love has turned his brain.

Dosie. [*Decisively.*] Where is he?

Van. In my room writing farewell letters to a few friends.

Dosie. [*Goes to door,* L., *and pushes it open, calls.*] Mr. Versus, will you step here a moment.

Tom *enters,* L., *an Indian crown of feathers on his head and a few in his hand.*

Tom. My goddess calls me.

Dosie. Just drop all those fancy names, and tell me plainly what all this means. [*Points to chest.*]

Tom. Only a few necessary articles to begin with. By Jove! I forgot, we shall require some canned tomatoes and some preserved peaches, and we want a bow string and a sack. [*Hurries to* L.] I must order them at once.

Dosie. Stop. [*He turns.*] You need not have taken these absurd means of letting me know that our union is distasteful.

Tom. My angel—

Dosie. Do you expect me to believe all this stuff about Ubjibbeloola, or whatever it is.

Tom. You said you'd follow me to the end of the earth, and I'm only going to the middle of it.

Dosie. I said as many foolish things as you did. I ought to have known that your making love to me was meant for some one else. I know it now. But you need not have resorted to such very strong measures to undeceive me. If you had said it was a mistake, I'd have said well and good, we'll say no more about it. But you acted like—well, no matter. You are free. You are free. [*Bursts into tears and exits,* R.]

Van. I knew she had sense, and it's coming out at last.

Tom. [*Takes off his crown, looks at it, and pitches it away.*] She ought to have boxed my ears.

Geagle. [*Outside.*] Run, I hear him. This way.

MARY FORREST *enters, followed by* GEAGLE, *who winks at everybody in delight.*

Geagle. [*Points to Van.*] There he is!

Mary. [*In great agitation.*] For Heaven's sake, tell me what has happened?

Mrs. V. Happened, child? Happened to whom?

Mary. To your son. Where is he?

Mrs. V. My son?

Mary. Don't you know. Hasn't Mr. Vandusen told you yet.

Mrs. V. [*Frightened, crosses to Van.*] What has become of Kit? I have not seen him to-day.

Mary. [*Gives her letter.*] Look! Your husband's message to me.

GEAGLE *enters at* C. *with* KIT, *restraining him.*

Mrs. V. [*Reads.*] "My Dear Miss Forrest: I am sorry to say that I cannot deliver your farewell message to my son, for the reason that I have a son no longer. Yours, C. Vandusen." [*To Van.*] What does it mean? You have a son no longer.

Van. No, because Geagle has adopted him. [GEAGLE *releases Kit, rushes down and dances a jig on box.*] Hurrah!

Kit. [*Rushes to Mary. She is so overcome that her head sinks on his shoulder, and he has to put his arm around her waist.*] You cannot deny it. You do love me. I may speak now. [*Draws her to* L.]

Mary. I'm so glad you are not dead. [*They go up.*]

Tom. I suppose I'd better go.

Geagle. No, you don't. [*Runs to* R., *and calls.*] Silena. [*Comes down.*] She made a match for me on this very spot, and I mean to give her tit for tat. [*Crosses to* R.]

Silena. [*Outside,* R. 1 E.] Papa!

Geagle. [*Goes to* R.] There she is.

SILENA *appears, led by* DOSIE, *who is radiant.* GEAGLE *retreats in alarm to* L. *corner.* SILENA *goes over to Tom.*

Dosie. Let me present Mr. Versus with the bride he really wanted.

Tom. [C.] Is it possible? [*Takes Silena in his arms.*]

Silena. You won't go to Africa now.

Tom. [*Holding her.*] No. It's quite warm enough here.

Dosie. [R. 1 E., *peeps across roguishly to Geagle. He glances timidly. She smiles. He is alarmed.*] Ahem!

Geagle. [*Aside.*] I don't like that. She can't mean to go for me again.

Dosie. Are you very much blighted, Mr. Geagle?

Geagle. Frost-bitten to the core.

Dosie. [*Beckons to him.*] He! he! [GEAGLE *shakes his head. She whispers.*] I want to speak to you.

Geagle. Say it right out.

Dosie. [*Advancing a few steps.*] Come over. [*He advances a step, then stops.*] I won't hurt you.

Geagle. Honor bright?

Dosie. [*Coming to* C., GEAGLE *also. Confidentially.*] We've been a couple of geese.

Geagle. Yes!

Dosie. But we've come to our senses at last.

Geagle. [*Doubtfully.*] You are sure about yourself?

Dosie.   For a time I felt as if I were a girl again.   Heigho!
It had all the freshness of May and the balminess of June.

Geagle.   I know.   It was our Indian summer—a sort of warm
spell late in the fall.

Dosie.   Poetic thought!   Ah!   [*Sighs and casts loving eyes at
him.*]

Geagle.   Ah!

Sil.   [*Mischievously interrupting.*]   Needles and pins!   [Dosie
and Geagle *retreat to their respective corners.*   Sil. *laughs.
All laugh.*]   I didn't mean to frighten—only to warn you.

Tom.   Oh! hang it, darling.   Remember, I'm just about to
get married.   Don't sing that old song.

Van.   No.   Give us something a little more cheerful.

Mrs. V.   Let Mr. Geagle express his feelings.

Mary.   And Miss Dosie.

Dosie.   Not before everybody.

Geagle.   Oh, yes!   I don't mind.   [*Steps forward.*]

Sil.   Something poetical!

Mrs. V.   Practical!

Van.   Historical!

Mary.   Æsthetical!

Kit.   Musical!

Tom.   Autobiographical!

Geagle.—

> Hey diddle, diddle, the cat and the fiddle—
> We wanted a late honeymoon!
> But the merry dogs laughed to see such sport,
> And the Miss ran away with the Spoon!

[*Indicates Silena and Tom.*]

Curtain.